Smooth Operator

The phone seemed to glow on the wall. The harder Mark tried to ignore it, the more it caught his eye. It beckoned to him.

With a sigh, Mark picked it up. He called the teen Party Line.

"Hello?" he said.

"This is private," a voice said. "Do you mind?"

The voice was low and deep. It sounded odd somehow. I know that voice, Mark thought. Not just from the Party Line. I've heard it somewhere else.

**Other Point paperbacks
you will enjoy:**

Party LINE

A. Bates

SCHOLASTIC INC.
New York Toronto London Auckland Sydney

ISBN 0-590-42439-4

12 11 10 9 8 7 6 5 4   9/8 0 1 2 3 4/9

Printed in the U.S.A.   01

First Scholastic printing, June 1989

*To Ainslie, of course, for always believing;
to Shayle, Alia, and Lisha, my best critics and
my inspiration.
And to Greg, for making it real.*

Chapter 1

The locker still wouldn't open. Scott looked at the piece of paper they'd given him in the office.

"Must be jammed," he muttered. "This is the right locker, and I'm trying the right combination."

He spun the dial again, stopping carefully at the numbers listed on the paper. Then he glanced quickly up and down the hall. The coast was clear. In one quick move he took a step back and kicked the center of the lock, smashing the latch upward. The door flew open and something red sprang from the locker towards his face. He ducked automatically.

For a second Scott couldn't breathe. Panic clogged his throat. His heart seemed to stop. Oh, no, he thought. For a second I could have sworn that was a bloody arm.

Then he screamed.

It WAS a bloody arm.

* * *

Mark scratched his head. What happens next? he asked himself. He tapped his pencil against his front teeth, thinking. He got a fresh piece of notebook paper and stared at it. It didn't help. He couldn't think what to write next.

Finally he crumpled the blank paper and flung it at the trash can next to the sink. I'm never going to get done at this rate, he thought. Mr. Santos is going to murder me if I don't hand something in this time. If I flunk English I'll just have to take it again and I couldn't stand another year of Santos!

He glanced again at the phone. It shone out from its place on the wall like it always did when Mark was home alone. It seemed like the largest, shiniest, most noticeable thing in the kitchen. It beckoned to him.

The next thing he knew, he was holding the receiver in his hand.

Feeling guilty, he dialed 976-TEEN-2, the bargain teen talk line, line 2. He could call any line from 1 to 4, fifty cents for the first minute, twenty-five cents for each minute after that. There was no charge unless someone else was on, too.

The line clicked and Mark was on.

"Hello?" he said.

"Hi. Who's this?" asked a female voice.

"Umm . . . Scott," Mark said.

"Hi, Scott. This is Steffie. Steve and Traci are on the line, too."

"This is Traci. We're talking about guys getting too fresh." Traci giggled. "Steffie says there's no such thing as too fresh, but I think she's being a tease."

"Are you teasing, Steffie?"

The voice was low and deep, so Mark figured it was Steve, the other guy on the line. He sounds odd, somehow, Mark thought.

"Maybe. Yeah, I guess I am," Steffie admitted.

"I'd like to call you," Steve said. "To talk to you some more."

"He's asking for your phone number," Traci said. "Are you giving it out?"

"Umm, not yet," Steffie said.

Mark heard a key scratching into the lock on the apartment door.

"Gotta go," he said. " 'Bye."

He hung up the phone and raced for his chair, sliding into the seat as he heard the door close.

"In here, Mom," he called. He scribbled furiously on the top piece of paper in the stack in front of him, crumpling it as his mother trudged into the room. He tossed the wad towards the trash can, adding it to the others he'd thrown.

"We're supposed to be writing a story," he explained. "For English. You look tired," he added.

"I am tired," his mother said. "My feet are starting to swell up from standing all night. It's a long walk home with swollen feet. I don't like walking home alone at night. It makes me nervous." She sighed. "Who'd have thought I'd end up as a clerk at Discount City?"

I know, I know, Mark thought. You were Miss

Spring Fever in 1854 or something. Maybe it was 1548. And voted Prettiest Girl in your class. And Miss Typist of the Year.

"Miss Typist, too," she went on. "And look at me now."

"We don't have it so bad," Mark said, feeling guilty about the phone bill he kept running up in spite of his promise not to. He wanted to make her smile. "We've got each other. What more could we want?"

She did smile, looking pleased.

She looks younger when she smiles, Mark thought. I guess she hasn't been smiling that much lately. And I guess she's not really so old. She looks a lot like me, too, he realized. Pale blue eyes, dark hair, curls.

"We could want a car," she said. But she kept smiling.

"Maybe you'll get better hours before it snows," he said.

"Maybe." She hung up her coat. "I'm going to have my bath and go to bed," she said. "Good night. And good luck on your story."

"I'm never going to be a writer!" Mark complained, crumpling another sheet of paper.

In a few minutes he heard the water running in the bathtub. His eyes strayed to the phone again.

Too risky, he decided. Sound carries too well in this place. After last month's bill, she'd kill me if she knew I was still calling. He looked glumly at the blank paper.

What would happen next? he asked himself

again. Scott would go for help, I guess. And when the people got to his locker, there wouldn't be any arm. Of course, the locker used to belong to somebody who got murdered. But Scott's a new kid and he doesn't know that.

Mark scribbled quickly, visions of bloody arm stumps, bloody knives and bloody bodies filling his imagination. He shivered. I'm scaring myself, anyway, he thought. Maybe this once Santos will give me a decent grade.

Chapter 2

The next morning, Friday, Mark joined Todd and Robbie for the walk to school. Together they grumbled about their assignments and compared their available cash, agreeing that their prospects were miserable in both departments. Then the talk shifted, inevitably, to girls.

"Did you see Gina this morning?" Todd asked. "Wow!"

"Wow what?" Mark asked. "She look good?"

"Yeah!" Todd said, his voice reverent.

"They all look good to you," Mark told him.

"I wish I had the nerve to ask one of them out," Todd said.

"All it takes is a little guts," Robbie said. "And everybody's got guts. If you cut your belly open, you'd find guts inside. Guaranteed."

"They don't do me much good, then," Todd admitted. "If I've got them, they're yellow."

Yellow guts, Mark thought. That's me, too.

"Now take me, for instance," Robbie said,

snapping himself on the chest. "I figure girls want guys as much as we want them. Makes sense, right? Otherwise, where would the world be? So if they want us, there's no problem."

"Maybe not for you," Todd said gloomily. "You're a jock. Girls like jocks."

"Girls like guys," Robbie corrected, emphasizing each word. "Besides, I'm not much of a jock this semester. Not until my grades improve. But look at the world, guys. I'm telling you, women go for men. Look at Mr. Santos. If you ask me, you couldn't find a bigger creep, but have you seen his wife? If he can get someone like her, you should have no problem, believe me!"

"Yeah, I suppose," Todd agreed. But he sounded doubtful.

Mark folded his jacket collar up around his neck. The late-September morning was chilly, the wind biting. Mark knew it would warm up later, with a hot and sunny afternoon. Most days were still warm, but it was definitely getting dark earlier. And the nippy mornings and evenings of the past week promised an early winter.

"Are you going to the dance tonight?" Todd asked them.

Mark shook his head.

"Why not?" Robbie asked. "I'm going. There will be girls there."

"The girls with dates will be there," Mark pointed out.

"There are always plenty of single girls, too," Robbie said.

"Sure. And they stand with a bunch of friends, so you feel like an idiot breaking into their little group," Mark said.

"And they probably won't dance unless someone asks the friends, too," Todd added.

Robbie shook his head. "You're right. You're a chicken," he told Todd. "But you're in good company. Mark's a chicken, too."

Mark scowled, but he didn't disagree. He wished he was more like Robbie, with confidence, and an easy, teasing way with girls. It seemed like Robbie always had girls around him.

Mark surprised his teacher by handing in the story he'd written.

"You're handing in an assignment the day it's due?" Mr. Santos said, acting amazed. "Is this the same Mark who's been in my class since the beginning of school? Or a doppelgänger who traded places with you in secret?"

That's just like Santos, Mark thought. Always has to have the last word. I'll bet he thinks I don't know a doppelgänger is a person's spirit twin. He loves to try to prove how smart he is.

Mark didn't answer Mr. Santos' comments. He settled back to listen to the lecture while still sparing adequate attention for the girls in the class. I wonder if any of them are the girls on the Party Line, he thought. Not Janet. She's too rich for a cut-rate line. If she calls, she'd use the expensive lines. And not Jenny. She wouldn't have the time. She's so popular already her phone probably never quits ringing. Kelly, too. What do girls like that need with a Party Line? Why should they pay for something they can get for free?

He kept watching people as he stepped out into the hall after his English class. Seems like all these guys know everybody else, he thought. I'll bet I'm the only one from this school who calls on the Line. You've got to be bored or lonely to call. These kids don't look bored or lonely.

At his locker, he opened the door slowly, feeling foolish when he realized he was waiting for a bloody arm to fall out. He grabbed his books and headed to his next class.

As usual, Robbie stayed after school for help with his math, and Todd took the bus over to the mall where he worked as a chicken fryer in a fast chicken-chip joint. Mark walked home alone, his jacket suspended from his thumb, hanging over his shoulder.

As soon as he'd eaten a fat tuna sandwich and gulped a glass of milk, he called. I'll try line 3 today, he decided.

"Hello!"

It was a guy's voice. It sounded vaguely familiar to Mark. "Uh, hi. Anybody else on?" Mark asked. Meaning girls, he thought.

"No."

" 'Bye then," Mark said. He tried line 4, dialing 976-TEEN-4.

"Hello?" said a female voice.

"Hi, this is Todd," Mark said. "Who's on?"

"This is Nicky."

"Hi, Nicky. Anybody else on?"

"Nope. Just us. How old are you?"

"Seventeen," Mark said. He smiled to himself. At least that's true, he thought. "How about you?"

"Fifteen. Is that too young?"

"Depends on what for, I guess," Mark said. "I mean, I guess fifteen sounds fine."

The sign-on tone sounded and a male voice said hello. Nicky said hi and the two asked the usual questions of each other while Mark listened. Nicky went to East High, Ben to Central. Ben was sixteen. He liked fifteen-year-old girls.

"Are you still on, Todd?" Nicky asked.

In the few seconds it took Mark to remember he'd given Todd's name, Nicky had said, "I guess not. It's just us, Ben."

Their conversation continued around him. It's the same guy, Mark decided. From line 3 a minute ago. And he was on last night. He said his name was Steve, then. That's why he sounded familiar. He's got as many names as I have.

Mark got bored listening, but didn't want to hang up. It was cheaper to stay on one line than to keep calling different ones. The first minute cost the most. Besides, he didn't want to give himself away by hanging up. That would make a sign-off tone, and they thought he'd already signed off. That could be embarrassing if he got either of them on a line again.

"I'd like to call you," Ben said. "Can I have your phone number?"

"Umm, no. I don't think so," Nicky said. "But

you could call me back on the Party Line, couldn't you?"

"It's not as private," Ben said. "But I guess it's better than nothing. Which line?"

"Line 4," Nicky said. "When?"

"Tonight?"

"Sure. I can call back at eight-thirty."

"I'll be waiting, darlin'."

They rang off, to Mark's relief. If he held the line now, he wouldn't be charged until another call came in. That was one nice thing about discount lines, they only charged for actual use time. Waiting for a call to log on to yours was free.

But after two guys logged on, one after the other, he gave up.

Slow this afternoon, he thought. I'll call back tonight. "Darlin'!" he snorted, mimicking Ben's voice.

Chapter 3

"Hi, who is this?"

"Robbie," said Mark.

"Hi, Robbie, I'm Janine."

"How're you doing?" he asked. "I think I talked with you a couple of weeks ago. You were having a pretty bad day."

"Yeah, well, that's the story of my life. One of these days I'll have my own place. Things will pick up then."

"Yeah, maybe," Mark agreed. "Is anyone else ɔn?"

"No," Janine told him. "I've been holding for nearly ten minutes. Kept getting Nicky. I've heard her before. Talking with some guy named Robert, mostly. Is that you?"

"No. Just Robbie. Not Robert."

"Oh. This time she wanted someone named Ben."

"Oh, yeah," Mark said. "I heard them earlier. I think he's going to call at eight-thirty."

"You want to know something I figured out?" Janine asked. "It's a trick."

"Yeah, sure."

"After you log in, hit 1, 9, and 7 together. That makes a disconnect tone. You know, that sign-off tone?"

"What good does that do?" Mark asked.

"I'm hoping it fools the computer," Janine said. "If it sounds like a sign-off to the people on the line, which it does, then maybe the billing computer is fooled, too. Maybe I won't have such a big bill next month."

"That would be great!" Mark said. "My mom hit the roof last month, and I didn't talk half as much as I have this month."

"It gets addictive," Janine agreed. "At first I just called to hear a friendly voice, and, you know, see what it was all about. And then I kept calling more and more."

"I know," Mark said. "I've called so often I'm starting to recognize people by their voices."

"Yeah, me too," Janine said.

"You ever wonder how much of what people say is true?" Mark asked. "Like their names and schools and stuff?"

"Yeah," Janine said. "I guess a lot of people lie."

"I did," Mark admitted. "My name is Mark, not Robbie."

Janine laughed. "I'm still Janine," she said. "And I don't remember telling any lies. But I bet a lot of kids do. Sometimes the truth is boring, I guess."

"Or else we are," Mark said. "I am, anyway. I call to talk, but I never have anything to say, so I wind up just listening."

The sign-on tone sounded.

"Hello?" Janine said. "Who is this?"

"Nicky," came the new voice.

"Still looking for Ben?" Janine asked.

"Yeah."

She sounded very young to Mark, more like thirteen than the fifteen she'd said she was. Mark felt sorry for her. She sounded so eager to get Ben on the line, and so disappointed when Janine answered.

"Hey, Nicky," he said. "I was on the line earlier, remember?"

"Yeah. Todd, right?"

Janine giggled.

"Yeah," Mark said. "Anyway, Ben said he'd call you at eight-thirty. Line 4."

"I thought you'd signed off," Nicky said.

"I just put the phone down," Mark lied. "I'd dropped something and I put the phone down to get it. When I picked the phone back up I heard you tell Ben you could call back at eight-thirty."

"Oh," Nicky said. "Well, I'm glad you heard because I forgot what I told him."

"Write it down," Mark advised. "Line 4, eight-thirty."

"Thanks!" Nicky said. " 'Bye."

" 'Bye," Mark and Janine told her.

"You've saved a romance," Janine said. "Hey, I gotta go. I've been on forever."

"Can I call you back?" Mark asked quickly.

"Sure. I'm on all the time," Janine said. " 'Bye."

"I meant, call you back at your home number," Mark explained. But the disconnect tone had already sounded. Mark hung up, too, then wondered if Janine had really signed off or if she'd just hit the 1-9-7 together.

Too late now, he thought. I'd better do some homework and stay off the phone. At least I don't have to write another story for a while.

He found a package of hot dogs in the fridge, along with a package of buns. "Dinner" read the note his mother had left. Only the note was on a foil-wrapped stick of Parkay.

It must have fallen from the hot dogs, Mark decided. I'm sure she doesn't expect me to eat margarine. Things can't be that bad. He cooked four hot dogs and ate them.

Then he unearthed his math book from the pile of things he'd dumped on the table and dropped onto the couch, another hot dog in hand. He was surprised when he finished his assignment easily. He double-checked his answers.

Math used to be harder than this, he thought. But this year I've been understanding everything. Maybe I'm better at math than I thought.

Janine sounded nice, he decided, stuffing his books back into his pack. I liked talking to her. And I actually talked instead of just listening. I wonder what she looks like. I don't even know if she's a blonde or brunette. She could have red hair, too, I guess. I'll have to ask her.

We didn't really say anything personal, he

thought. Though I guess that's what happens on the Line. I've listened to enough conversations to know. People talk a lot, but they don't usually give out personal information.

At least, not right away, he decided. Maybe they do later. After they've talked a few times. Maybe once they feel like getting personal they give out their phone numbers and go on from there on their own lines.

He sighed. He wondered if he was hungry enough to eat the rest of the hot dogs. He decided he was. He wandered into the kitchen and put the hot dogs in a pan to fry. He loaded the buns with mustard, ketchup and relish, then assembled the hot dogs.

He had to walk by the phone to reach the table.

The phone seemed to gleam on the wall and the harder he tried to ignore it, the more it caught his eye.

With another sigh, Mark picked it up. He called.

Chapter 4

Line 4. It was almost nine. Nicky and Ben were on the line.

"This is private," Ben's voice said. "Do you mind?"

Not even a "hi" first, Mark thought. He punched 1-9-7 at the same time and heard the tone. Janine was right, he thought. It sounds just like the sign-off tone.

He wasn't actually interested in Nicky and Ben's conversation, but he thought it served Ben right to have someone eavesdrop after Ben had been so rude.

"So, darlin', what do you look like?" Ben asked. "You can tell me that, can't you?"

"I'm about five-five," Nicky said. Mark thought she sounded sweet and shy, and very young. "I weigh 110 pounds. I have brown hair. It's curly. Blue eyes."

"Light brown hair, sweetheart?" Ben asked. "Or dark brown?"

I know his voice, Mark thought. Not just from

the Party Line. I've heard it somewhere else. I wonder how many of these people I know. I'll bet I know lots of them.

"Light brown," Nicky said. "Is that okay?"

"Why, of course it's okay. It's wonderful. And what do you like to do? Ride horses? Bike? Hike?"

"I like to take long walks," Nicky said.

"That sounds like fun. Where do you walk? In the country? Or to the mall or something?"

"Mostly I walk in this field," Nicky said. "It's a big field, with a bumpy path around the edge near where the irrigation ditch runs. I see pheasants, even. And sometimes I hear that bird — I think it's a meadowlark. Its song is so beautiful! It's sad and happy at the same time. Kind of like me, maybe."

"That's nice, darlin'. I'd like to hear those birds, too."

"You'd like them, I bet," Nicky said. "I like to think they're telling me things will be okay."

The sign-on tone sounded for another caller.

"This is private, do you mind?" Ben said.

"Yeah, I do mind," the new caller said. "I'm expecting a call on this line."

Mark thought the new voice sounded faintly familiar, too, though he couldn't place it. It doesn't matter, he thought. One thing I know for sure is as long as Ben and Nicky and I are all on the line with the last caller, whoever he's expecting won't be able to get through. Four calls are all each line can handle.

"I have to go anyway," Nicky said.

"Can I call you again?" Ben asked.

"Yeah. Keep trying line 4," Nicky said. "I can probably call back later tonight."

"If I had your number, I could call you any time," Ben said.

"No," Nicky said. "My folks wouldn't like that. But try later tonight, okay? I can call back around ten. We'll talk more then. I really have to go. 'Bye." She rang off.

Ben cursed once, then rang off.

Mark hung up, too, feeling a little guilty for eavesdropping. Even if he mostly used the Party Line to listen to other people talk, at least before, they'd known he was on the line.

That Ben was sure angling for information from Nicky, Mark thought. Of course, I guess that's what we all want. To get close to girls.

He sighed. I'm bored, he thought. I want to do something. It's too dark to play basketball. I wonder if anything's on TV.

He turned on the set and flipped through the channels. All the shows had already started, and he couldn't get interested in figuring out the story lines.

I hate Friday night TV, he thought. Early news, a family comedy, educational TV, a news magazine show, reruns of that detective show, a religious program and some dumb secret agent movie. Dumb shows for dummies, because only dummies stay home and watch TV on Friday nights.

Especially when the dummy could be at a

dance instead, he reminded himself. Being bored at a dance would be better than being bored watching stupid shows on TV. Besides, it's barely nine-thirty. Things would just be warming up.

Chapter 5

He nodded to the music, watching sideways out of the corner of his eye. The two girls standing to his left wore jean skirts. One had on a short-sleeved sweater and high-top sneakers, one wore a striped blouse and dressier shoes. They kept whispering together, but Mark couldn't tell what they were saying, he could just hear the rise and fall of their voices.

Robbie came by and draped a ribbon of crepe paper around Mark's neck like a tie.

"Hey," Robbie said. "Glad you decided to come. Good move. Guess what? I got a job this afternoon. Teaching."

"You? Teach?" Mark asked. "What?"

"Auto mechanics. At the rec center on Saturdays. If I can save enough money, I'm going to get me a car."

"They pay you?"

"Not much," Robbie admitted. "But some. And I meet girls."

"In an auto mechanics class?"

Robbie grinned. "You'd be surprised," he said. He handed Mark a folded sheet of paper. "See? I'm even listed," he said. "Except not my name."

Mark looked at the paper. It was a rec center schedule.

"Mmm," Robbie said. "I think that girl over there wants to dance with me. See you."

Mark folded the schedule and stuck it in his pocket. Robbie was glad to see me, anyway, he thought, watching the pattern of people as they formed groups and couples, shifted and re-formed.

It wasn't Homecoming, or any special occasion. Just a dance. But the gym had been decorated with crepe paper streamers and balloons. Two corners were lit, with the lights aiming up and diagonally across the room, roughly towards the two unlit corners. The big sound system had been set up and kids hung around the console, thumbing through tapes and albums.

This is better than TV, Mark told himself, but they're the same in one obvious way. I watch both of them.

One of the girls who'd been standing to his left moved nearer.

"You're Mark Carney," she said. "You're in my math class. Only I sit in the back. You probably don't see me."

Mark turned his head to look at her. "Yeah, I've seen you," he said. "You're Marcy, right?"

She smiled, seeming pleased that he knew her name.

"Yeah. Marcy Nehrman. How come you're in that math class?"

"What do you mean?"

"Don't tell me you didn't know we're in the dummy class?"

Mark shrugged. "I hadn't realized," he said. "It seemed awfully easy this year. I guess I figured I just got smart."

Marcy laughed at him, but it was a nice laugh. "I can tell the class is easy for you," she said. "You always know the answers. I'll bet they move you up pretty soon."

"I guess I'll see how smart I am if they put me in a harder class," Mark told her. "But it'll be a shock to have to work. I kind of like finishing my homework in fifteen minutes."

"Yeah, right," Marcy agreed.

She stood near him in silence for a few minutes, then shrugged and walked off. Mark was disappointed. Then he heard someone behind him.

"You dummy! Why didn't you ask her to dance?"

It was the other girl, the one who'd been standing with Marcy. Mark recognized her now that he could see her better. She was in his English class. Libby something.

"Me?" Mark asked.

"Who else was she talking to?" Libby said. She sounded disgusted. "Guys are so dumb. Or isn't she pretty enough for you?"

"Marcy?" Mark asked, feeling stupider and

stupider. "Of course she's pretty. She's nice, too."

"So she comes up to you. She talks to you. And you stand there like a dolt." Libby rolled her eyes in disgust and walked off.

Mark felt like he'd stumbled into a warp of some kind. Not a time warp, for the time hadn't changed. And the room was familiar. He knew the people, he spoke the language. But the words didn't mean what he thought they meant.

I AM a dolt, he thought. If I've got this figured out right, Marcy was telling me she'd dance with me if I asked, and I was too stupid to understand.

He wondered if it was too late to find Marcy and ask her to dance. He wondered if he had enough guts to find Marcy and ask her to dance. He wondered if he would always be stupid or if he'd get smarter as time went on.

He looked around the gym, trying to see where Marcy had gone. He wished he was standing with a couple of other guys instead of all alone. It looked more interesting to be in a group. At least those people had someone to talk to.

I could still ask someone to dance, he finally realized. There are lots of girls standing around. But maybe they don't want to dance. If they don't, why are they here? Maybe they just don't want to dance with me. Anyway, if I ask someone to dance, and Marcy sees me, she'll think I specifically didn't want to dance with her, 'cause there I am, dancing with someone else when I didn't ask her. That would hurt her feelings.

Finally, feeling totally confused, he left.

Chapter 6

Mark was almost halfway home when he heard the footsteps behind him.

He looked around, suddenly nervous.

There was no one there.

I am not going to run, he told himself. I'm just scaring myself. There's no one there. No one is following me.

The night sounds seemed to amplify, becoming sharper, echoing and rapping, crackling and slithering. The air seemed like a mass, a fog that he had to push his way through. Somewhere behind him, a twig snapped.

Mark walked faster. He couldn't seem to catch his breath.

This is so dumb, he told himself. But he couldn't seem to keep from walking even faster.

If only he could make it to the end of the block. There was light at the end of the block. This town could use more streetlights, he thought. It would be safer.

A dog barked outside the house to his left, and he jumped, jerking violently.

Then he heard the footsteps again. And a strange, squeaking noise.

He stepped into the ring of light cast by a streetlight at the end of the block. He realized he'd been holding his breath and let it out in a slow gasp. From here home, porch lights, business nightlights and streetlights would pave the way.

I will walk in the light, he thought, grinning because it reminded him of the TV evangelists.

You idiot! he told himself. You're not eight years old anymore. You're a big boy now, and you don't need lights to get home safely.

But he was still relieved.

All of a sudden the lights went out — all of them — like candles on a birthday cake.

What's happening? he thought wildly. Is it a blackout? A power failure?

The squeaky sound emerged from the darkness. It was a voice. It was right behind him.

It was so real and so immediate that he spun around, looking for whomever had spoken.

"Mark . . . " said the voice. "You have my arm. I want it back."

This better be a joke, thought Mark. He started running. Robbie? he thought. Todd?

His feet weren't moving. They felt as if they were stuck in tar . . . like they were glued to the sidewalk and he couldn't lift them enough to get away.

He looked behind him again, and saw a man's figure. A man with only one arm.

"Mark!" the man hissed. "I have something for you! I found it! I found my arm! I'll share it with you."

Only then did Mark see the stump of a bloody arm, clutched in the man's good hand. He was raising the stump to strike Mark with.

Mark looked up. The bloody arm was beginning to descend. He looked straight into the man's face and saw . . .

"Mr. Santos!" gasped Mark, sitting suddenly upright in bed.

He looked around. What? he thought.

I'm home. I'm in my own bed. I'm safe. I'm safe!

He shook his head to clear away the nightmare.

No more walking home alone in the dark, he promised himself. No more whole packages of hot dogs for dinner. And . . . no more horror stories for Mr. Santos. Ever!

Chapter 7

"I don't know," she said. "Maybe I stink and don't know it. But nobody's ever said so."

"You don't stink. Guys stink. They're just so stupid."

Mark thought of them as girl number 1 and girl number 2, though he thought girl number 2 sounded a little like Marcy's friend Libby, the girl who'd called him a dummy at the dance the night before.

He'd called in, then faked the sign-off signal when he realized the girls were discussing guys. It had taken a lot of nerve to call in at all with his mother in the other room. But she'd seemed so engrossed in the paper Mark decided it was safe to call as long as he didn't say anything. He was still nervous, though. Not only was he eavesdropping, it was also the first time he'd ever called the Line with anyone nearby.

But I NEED to hear this, he thought. I can learn something. And I NEED to learn something about girls. At the rate I've been going,

I'll be eighty before any girl even lets me hold her hand.

"What is so hard about being nice?" girl number 1 asked. "I'd be happy if guys just smiled at me. I'd feel like I was at least okay. They walk by me like I don't even exist. They look at the ground or the walls instead of me. The only guys who even talk to me are the guys on the Line — who can't see me! That's great for the ego, you know?"

And that's it, Mark thought. Invisibility. That's the whole secret here. We can open up to people on the Line because they can't really see us at all. It's almost like a dream world where we just imagine the other people, except they talk out loud to us. We're all invisible and safe, but if we met face to face we wouldn't be invisible anymore.

"I know," number 2 said glumly. "Same here. I can't be that bad! But they don't even look. Why do I bother getting up early and curling my hair and stuff? It obviously isn't doing any good. Guys just don't notice."

We notice! Mark thought. We notice! Honest we do. We're just too chicken to do anything about it. You think we're looking at the walls and the floors? We're looking at you! We're just trying to look without anybody knowing it.

But he didn't say a word out loud.

"I wonder if they'd notice if we went to school looking awful? All frizzy-haired or something," number 1 said.

Number 2 giggled. "Yes, they would. They'd

definitely notice then! They'd even look at us in the halls. The problem is, no matter how good we looked after that they'd remember us forever as the frizzy-haired creature. No thanks. That's not how I want to be remembered."

"Isn't SOME kind of attention better than none?" number 1 asked.

Number 2 sighed. "Maybe," she said. "Do you think I should just whack one of them upside the head? Would he notice me then?"

It really sounds like Libby, Mark thought. I wonder if it is. There's got to be a lot of kids from school calling in. Libby could be one of them. Even if it seems like a dream world, these aren't imaginary people on the Line, not ghosts. They're just as real as I am.

"That might not be too bad an idea," number 1 said. "I bet a lot of guys would notice you if you whacked them on the head."

"It's just so unfair!" number 2 said. "Guys don't do anything special — just take a shower and put on clothes. And we notice them. Then we spend forever with hair dryers and curling irons and makeup and it isn't enough. I don't know what to do."

"Maybe I'm just not pretty enough," number 1 said glumly. "But if we have to be perfect to get a guy's attention I'll never make it."

"It's depressing," number 2 agreed.

"So what do we do?"

"Don't ask me," number 2 said. "If I knew the answers I wouldn't be sitting home alone talking to you. I just don't understand guys."

"Me, either," number 1 said, sighing.

"It would be so nice to be smiled at," number 2 said. "Just once. And to have guys say hi when they see me. It would be nice to go do something with a guy, too. I'm not asking for a fancy date. Just walking together and talking would be fun."

"I gotta go," number 1 said. "Listen, if you try anything and it works, let me know, okay?"

"Yeah. Same here."

They signed off. Mark hung up, too. Robbie said girls like guys, he thought. Maybe he's right. But why do I have to listen to a conversation on the Party Line to find it out?

Maybe because that's the only place they feel comfortable saying it, he thought. Because it's so anonymous. You make contact with other people, but on your own terms. No matter what you say, you aren't revealing any more of yourself than you want to reveal. It's safe.

He thought about the conversation, wondering if the girl could really have been Libby.

Probably not, he decided.

I wonder if I could find out?

Chapter 8

Monday morning Mark was summoned to the counselor's office and switched to a more advanced math class.

He was pleased with the change because it meant the teacher had realized he was able to do more difficult work, but it had been his only class with Marcy.

He watched for her in the halls between classes, but he didn't see her all morning.

In English, Mr. Santos handed back the stories the class had written . . . all except Mark's.

"Fear is an interesting part of being human," said Mr. Santos. "Humans experience all kinds and degrees of fear. Take phobias, for example. A phobia is like an obsession. It's an extreme, irrational fear. Then there's a group of common fears, like fear of the dark, of insects, of speed, of heights, of strangers, of being hurt. Those fears help us live safely. They're sensible fears. At least they are if we use them wisely, and it's pretty obvious how they can be used wisely."

He wrote *fight/flight* on the board. "Fear releases adrenalin, and adrenalin makes you feel high. People like feeling high."

Everyone in the class chuckled.

"Obviously, this is a protective mechanism, readying us to fight or flee, whichever we rationally decide is appropriate. But it's also fun."

He wrote *natural high* on the board. "That's why people like being scared," he said. "And why Halloween is so much fun. It's not only fun because people can dress up as any character they want and because they can go around getting candy, but also because it scares them. It's a safe, controlled fear. And people LIKE to be afraid — safely afraid, afraid in a controlled way. That's why Stephen King sells so many books and why there's a constant market for horror movies."

He picked up a few pieces of paper from his desk. "I hope you had fun with this assignment," he said. "I hope you learned a little bit about controlling fear, too, but mostly it was supposed to be fun. I'd like to read you one story. I know this author had fun. It shows in every paragraph. By the way, I'll smooth out the content and grammar as I read. The writing was a little rough, but I think you'll agree it's a great example of using and controlling fear."

He read.

Mark listened to his story. Coming from someone else it sounded different from when he'd read it to himself. Mr. Santos put a lot of expression into it, and the story took on sharper tones and darker undertones than Mark had realized were there. He found himself fascinated, caught up in his own work.

" 'She turned,' " Mr. Santos read, nearing the end of the story. " 'Scott held her hand tightly. They faced him together. He was a man, but his shadow, his size, his hatred made him a monster. His eyes were dark, but in the dim light, shining with crazed glee, they shone red. He came closer, step by step. The steps should have rung out on the pavement but they were only muted thuds. He raised his arm, the stump, holding it in his other hand. It came crashing down, not in slow motion but with a demon's blurred speed.

" 'It's over, Scott thought. At last it's over.' "

The kids let out a slow sigh as if they'd held their breaths in unison.

Wow, Mark thought. I can't believe I wrote that!

Mr. Santos advanced through the desks, stopping in front of Mark's.

"I have something for you," he said, and Mark shivered, reminded of his dream. Mr. Santos dropped the story on Mark's desk. Mark could see a bright red A + on the top of the first page.

A +! he thought. I've never gotten one of those before! Not on anything!

"Good job," Mr. Santos said. "Your spelling stinks, but there are a lot of spelling-check programs available for computers these days. Your grammar and punctuation could use some serious help, too. But with a little work and with a good editor you could be the next Edgar Allan Poe."

Mark slid down in his seat, his face burning.

"Don't get too excited," Mr. Santos said. "It's only one great story. That doesn't make you a great writer — yet. You still have a long way to go."

Mark looked down at his paper. He wasn't surprised Mr. Santos had to have the last word — again. And he wasn't at all sure, after his nightmare, that he ever intended to write another horror story. He had just two questions, though he didn't ask either one aloud.

He knew who Stephen King was, but who was Edgar Allan Poe?

And had he written anything lately?

Chapter 9

Mark's fame as an author spread quickly. By noon he had people he didn't even know stopping him in the halls to tell him their horror fantasies so he could use the ideas to write his first book.

"See, this guy gets in a fight, and when he slugs the other guy, every place he hits, the other guy's skin splits open and spiders come falling out, climbing all over. . . ."

"This girl goes home to visit her father over spring break and every night the father makes a little cut on her arm while she's sleeping. He slices the back of her arm, where she can't see it, and then he licks the blood off. She can't figure out why she's so tired every morning, and why her arm hurts. . . ."

"This guys works at the zoo, and he can't figure out why the monkeys always have bloody cages each morning, and why they're not hungry when he feeds them. . . ."

"Enough!" Mark told them, holding his arms

up to protect himself. "I'll never be able to sleep again."

The attention felt great, though Mark wasn't comfortable being praised. It embarrassed him. But he thought about the conversation he'd overheard on the Party Line.

He made himself smile, look people in the eye, and watch the girls instead of flushing and staring at the floor.

Most of the faces were pleasant, interested, and familiar, and slowly Mark realized he didn't have any reason to feel shy. These kids are okay, he thought. Even the girls.

He also made it a point to say hi to everyone he knew, especially the girls, when he passed them in the halls, surprised at how many people he felt comfortable talking to. I know a lot more people than I thought, he realized.

At lunch he sat with Todd, as usual, trading two of his peanut butter sandwiches for two of Todd's sliced turkey. He lined up his cookies, his apple and a banana, examining them critically, trying to decide which to eat first.

"I hear you're famous," Todd said, taking a huge bite of one of the peanut butter sandwiches.

"Yeah," Mark agreed. "All I need now is my fortune. Aren't they supposed to come together, fame and fortune?"

"They only come together to those who are humble." Libby, Marcy's friend from the dance, smiled at Mark and slid in next to Todd. "That lets you out."

Marcy slid in next to Mark. She smiled at him,

too, shyly, looking almost as if she expected him to slide away.

Mark gave her a grin. She's going to give me another chance! he thought. I won't blow it this time, honest!

Todd flushed. He stared at his lunch, unable to continue eating it. Mark couldn't help realizing he'd have reacted the same way, himself, if he hadn't overheard the girls on the Party Line. Now that he could see Todd's behavior from a different perspective, he had to admit it seemed unfriendly and disinterested, rather than shy and uncomfortable.

"How many people are you feeding?" Libby asked, looking from Todd's four sandwiches to Mark's four sandwiches.

Mark picked up the one he'd started eating and took a bite. "We're still growing," he said. As if waiting for an example to follow, Todd took another bite of his own lunch.

Marcy was small and dark, with short, dark brown hair that curled away from her face. She had on a white knit short-sleeved sweater and a pair of snug jeans. Libby was taller than Marcy, and had light brown hair pulled back and held by clips. She, too, wore snug jeans, and a striped T-shirt.

Mark thought they looked great.

"Trade you my cookies for your chips," he told Marcy.

She looked over at his lunch, frowning thoughtfully. "I'm tempted," she said.

"They're homemade," Mark said.

"I'm wavering," Marcy said.

"Chocolate chip," Mark said.

"Sold!" Marcy told him, tossing over her chips.

Mark handed her the baggie of cookies, making sure to smile and to look right at her. She smiled back. He noticed that Todd was still staring at his food, though he was taking little bites now and then. He'd almost finished his first sandwich.

"It was a good story," Libby said, talking to Mark, but only glancing at him once. She kept looking sideways at Todd.

She's interested in him, Mark realized. The signals are so clear when you know them.

"Thanks," he told Libby. "The problem is, it's the first and only complete story I've ever written. And the absolute only good one. What do I do for an encore?"

"That was your first story?" Libby asked. "How come it turned out so good, then?"

"I don't know," Mark admitted. "I just kept thinking of what would scare me, and that's what I wrote."

Marcy shivered. "Libby told me all about it," she said. "It would scare me, too! I'll never be able to open my locker again without being on the lookout for bloody arms."

"I know," Mark said. "I've got the same problem. And since I wrote that, I keep looking over my shoulder when I'm walking alone at night."

"I never walk alone at night," Marcy told him. "I'd be too scared to do it even if my parents would let me. They won't, though. They'd kill me if I ever did. They don't even like it if I walk alone during the day."

"You can't blame them," Libby said. "Have you been reading the papers? Three girls disappeared in broad daylight. In just the past few months. Here, I mean. In this city alone. It's scary!"

"Did they find any of them?" Todd asked.

Libby shook her head. "Not yet," she said.

"Maybe there's a one-armed maniac loose," Marcy said.

"Let's hope not," Mark told her.

"Maybe they ran away," Todd said.

"They could have," Libby said. "But none of them took anything with them. No money, no clothes, no food. Who would run away without clothes and money?"

"Did they leave notes?" Todd asked.

Libby shook her head again.

"You know, I really resent being vulnerable," Marcy said. "I don't like being afraid. I don't like having to walk with someone else for safety, even on my own street, in my own neighborhood. It's ugly."

"Take a self-defense class," Todd suggested.

"That's not a bad idea," Marcy said. "In fact, you two probably ought to take one, too. Guys may not be victimized as often, but it still happens."

"Mr. Santos said we could use fear to be safer," Libby said thoughtfully. "Using fear to get myself enrolled in a class just might be very sensible."

"Hey!" Mark said, slapping his back jeans pocket. "I've got a rec center schedule." He pulled it out. "Maybe they've got a class. Maybe we could all take it."

Mark turned to the schedule of classes, spreading the paper out so they could all see it.

"Look!" Marcy said, laughing. "They do have one. It's called, 'Fight Dirty and Live.' That's great!"

"When does it start?" Libby asked.

"Says it's ongoing," Todd pointed out. "Join any time."

"Saturday night?" Marcy said, wrinkling her nose. "Who wants to spend Saturday night taking classes?"

"I can't think of anything in my life it would interfere with," Libby said. "And anyway, it's from four-thirty to five-thirty. That's not exactly Saturday night. More like afternoon."

"How much?" Mark asked.

"Three dollars per session," Libby said. "Cheaper than a movie."

"I think it's a good idea," Todd said. "I wouldn't mind knowing how to fight dirty."

"Me, neither," Marcy said suddenly. "I'm game if you guys are. I don't want to do it alone."

"I kind of like the idea," Mark said.

"Are we going to do it or not?" Libby asked. "I want a firm, definite answer. I don't want to psych myself up for this and then be the only one who shows."

"I'll do it. Definitely," Mark said.

"Me, too," Marcy said. "If you'll walk over

with me, Libby. I'm sure either your mom or mine will give us a ride home."

"If I can get the car, I can give you a ride home," Todd offered quickly.

"Does that mean you'll do it, too? You'll take the class?" Libby asked.

"Yes. I'll take the class. I don't know how often I can get the car, though."

"We can work out the details," Marcy told him.

"Hey," Mark whispered to Marcy. "Thanks for taking another chance on me. I felt like a real idiot after the dance. I'm sorry I was so stupid."

"Don't thank me," Marcy said. "I was ready to give up on you, but Libby convinced me to try one more time."

After the girls left, Mark and Todd grinned at each other.

"I think I'm in love," Todd said.

"With who? Libby or Marcy?"

"Either. Both. I don't care. I have a date!"

Chapter 10

As Mark got ready for bed that night he realized
with a shock that he hadn't called the Party Line
all day. Not once.

That's a record, he thought. One whole day
without it.

By Wednesday afternoon he still hadn't called.
He wondered what was happening with the people
he knew on the Line. Even if they were just
voices and sometimes seemed shadowy and un-
real, they still seemed like friends. He also wondered what Janine was up to.

He stood for a full minute after he got home,
his hand on the phone. Finally he picked up the
receiver. He hit 1-9-7 as soon as he was logged
on.

"Hi and good-bye," he heard. He almost said
hi back because he recognized Janine's voice.
Darn! he thought. Should I go ahead and say hi
anyway?

"We're still alone, then," a male voice said.
"Like I said, Janine, I love your voice. Tell me

more about yourself. I want to be able to picture you while we're talking."

It sounds a little like that Ben person, Mark thought.

"I'm kind of tall," Janine said. "I'm five feet ten, Robert. That's pretty tall for a girl."

"I love looking up to women," Robert said. "Only, I'm six feet tall, so I've got you by two inches."

Me, too, Mark thought. I'm almost six feet, anyway.

"I have dumb brown hair," Janine said.

"Now why is it dumb to have brown hair?"

"It isn't," Janine said. "But my hair isn't brown. It's dumb brown. Like it couldn't decide whether to be blonde or brown so it did something in between. It's just dumb brown. Pale, but not blonde, and not dark enough to really be brown."

"Sounds pretty to me," Robert said. "What else?"

And you sound full of it to me, Mark thought.

"Kind of greenish eyes," Janine told him. "Nothing special."

"You shouldn't even think that," Robert said. "Of course you're special! You sound sensitive and kind and smart. You're the kind of girl any guy would want to meet."

"Yeah?" Janine said.

Mark couldn't tell for sure, but he thought Janine was trying not to laugh.

"I'd like to meet you," the guy said.

Mr. Santos! Mark thought suddenly. That's

who it sounds like! No wonder he showed up in my dream! I must have recognized the voice even though I didn't realize it. What a jerk! Why would a teacher call a teen line? Especially a married teacher!

The add-on tone sounded.

"Hello? Who's there?" Janine asked.

"I'm looking for Kerri," a boy's voice said.

"She's not on this line," Robert said. "But I am. I was having a private conversation."

The boy signed off.

"Why don't you give me your number at home so we can talk without interruption?" the guy said smoothly.

"I never give out my number," Janine said.

"Never?"

"I haven't yet," she said. "Maybe I will some day, if someone sounds interesting enough."

"And I don't?" he asked, sounding hurt.

"Not yet," Janine said.

"Well, I'm sorry I wasted your time," he said. The sign-off tone sounded.

"Hi, Sensitive, Kind and Smart," Mark said.

"Mark!" Janine sounded pleased. "I never should have told you my trick! I've turned you into an eavesdropper."

"Do you know how to make the sign-on tone?" he asked. "I'd have added myself back on, but I didn't know how."

"Good question," she said. "I'll have to play around with it and see if I can figure out a sign-on for you. Sneak!"

"You're the kind of girl any guy would want

to meet," Mark said, grinning to himself.

"Were you on from the beginning? Someone signed on and then signed right back off. That was you?"

"Yeah. I heard Mr. Smooth-Talker trying his moves on you. I hear people like that all the time, like the guy Nicky was trying to connect with the other day. This guy could be his twin."

"I know," Janine said. "He's got to be the same Robert I've heard Nicky talking to. He's determined, I'll give him that. I've missed you, Mark. What have you been doing instead of Party Lining?"

"Improving my life," Mark said. He told Janine about his story and the self-defense classes he was going to take, though he didn't mention Marcy. "I swear that guy you were talking to sounds just like my English teacher," he added. "Why would a teacher call a teen line?"

"He didn't sound old enough to be a teacher," Janine said. "But he did sound too eager. And he really passed out the compliments."

"Does that mean you wouldn't like me if I said you were the kind of girl any guy would like to meet?" Mark said.

Janine laughed. "You already did. But you're welcome to try it again. You never can tell. It might work this time."

"Actually I think you sound like you'd be fun," Mark said. "Easy to talk to. And I would like to meet you."

There was a long silence. Finally Janine said,

"I'm a chicken, Mark. What if you don't like me in person?"

"And what if I do?" Mark asked. "There's that possibility, too, you know. Besides, YOU might not like ME."

"Where would we meet?" Janine asked. "What would we do?"

"I've got the perfect spot to meet," Mark said. "How about meeting at church?"

"For real?" Janine asked.

"We don't have to go in," Mark said. "But meet me at St. Mark's, okay? Isn't that appropriate? It's that big church downtown with the gold spire, on Fifth and Curtis."

"I know it. When?"

"Sunday morning, eleven," Mark said. "We'll hold hands and walk and talk and feed the chipmunks in the park."

"You bring the chipmunk food," Janine said. "I'll bring the people food."

"How will I know you?" Mark asked. "Do you really have dumb brown hair and greenish eyes and are you really five ten or were you lying to oily-eager whoever it was?"

Janine laughed again. "I'm almost five nine," she said. "I exaggerated a little. But my hair is dumb brown and my eyes are greenish and you'll know me because I'll wear a blue sweater. And I'll have my jacket. It's checkered."

"Okay," Mark agreed. "And Janine?"

"Yeah?"

"Thanks." He smiled, even though she couldn't see him, and hung up the phone.

Chapter 11

Saturday morning while his mother walked to the grocery store Mark cleaned the apartment. He scrubbed the kitchen floor, lugged laundry downstairs to the building's washroom and started the machines, then straightened, dusted and vacuumed while the laundry washed. He'd just finished folding the clothes when his mother returned.

Mark helped carry groceries upstairs and put them away.

"No Oreos?" he asked, disappointed.

"I baked cookies last week, and I'm going to do it again this week," she said. "I'll bet you don't even remember that I used to do it all the time."

"Can you make Oreos?" Mark asked.

"I'm making chocolate chip again," she said firmly. "You will love them."

"They were good," Mark said, not mentioning that he'd traded some away. "Why this sudden attack of baking fever?"

"Because I'm tired of being too tired to do

anything," she said. "I'm tired of being in a rut. I work. I come home. I'm tired, so I take a bath and go to bed. I spend a lot of time feeling sorry for myself, watching TV and working. That's my entire life. But things are going to be different. I've decided life's too short to spend as a clerk at Discount City."

Mark poured a glass of milk for himself and a cup of coffee for his mother, carrying them both over to the table.

"I've decided it's time for a few changes," she went on. "First, I want a car."

"Me, too," Mark said.

"I've decided it's too dangerous to walk home alone at night around here. Just look at the paper! If I find a cheap enough car, can you fix it up?"

Mark quit shredding the napkin he'd used to dab up some drops of milk. He wadded it into a ball, rolling it between his palms. "I can do some," he said. "Depends on how bad off it is, I guess. I can do tune-ups and brakes, adjust the clutch and do all the easy stuff like replacing belts and hoses. I can't do transmissions. I can't rebuild engines."

"Could you pick a car that won't need that kind of work?" she asked. "I mean, can you tell if the engine is good, and the transmission and drive shaft?"

I didn't even know she'd ever heard of drive shafts, Mark thought, surprised. "I can catch obvious problems. But I've got a friend, Robbie. He teaches auto mechanics at the rec center. He knows a lot more than I do and I'll bet we could hire him to do the work I couldn't."

His mother looked relieved. "Good!" she said. "I was worried about getting stuck with an expensive lemon. Would you ask him if he knows of any cars for sale cheap?"

"Sure. How cheap?"

"Let's see," his mother said. "We have to put some aside for insurance. The license plates shouldn't be much for an old car. I'd say we've got between three and five hundred. I know that isn't much for a car, but it should buy something."

"It would have to be a real clunker!" Mark said.

"I wouldn't care, if it runs and gets me to work and back this winter. That's what I care about. It doesn't have to be pretty."

"I'll ask Robbie," Mark said, finishing his milk. "It never hurts to ask."

"Thanks," she said. "The second thing I've decided is to get a better job. Miss Typist of the senior class should qualify for something better than Discount City clerk. Right?"

"Sure," Mark told her. "You haven't explained the cookies, though."

"That's part of number three," she said, grinning. "I'm going to start doing things."

"Things?"

She nodded. "Bake cookies. Start jogging. Meet men. Take a class or two."

"Sounds ambitious," Mark said. "But I like the cookie part. Even if they aren't Oreos. Have you finished with the newspaper?"

"I need the want ads," she said. "You can have the rest of it."

Mark took the paper. On the front page was a three-column color photo of a young girl. Mark read the caption. *Nicoletta Marie Youngfield, 13-year-old daughter of Frank Youngfield, mayor of Longley, has been missing since last Friday night when she apparently left the house for a short walk some time late that evening.*

Something tickled at Mark's brain but he couldn't pinpoint what was bothering him.

Wait a minute! he thought. Nicoletta . . . Nicky? No, not Nicky! It can't be!

He scanned the article, reading quickly, hoping something would convince him he was wrong.

"She loved taking long walks alone," her father was quoted as saying. "There was a field near our house where she especially loved to walk. She talked a lot about the birds and animals she saw there."

The article said volunteers had searched the field, but had found no trace of the missing girl.

Mark felt sick. He remembered Nicky on the Party Line talking about walking in the field, listening to the meadowlarks. She'd seemed so young, kind of dreamy and shy.

"What's wrong?" his mother asked. Her voice was worried and Mark realized she'd asked him at least once already.

"I'm not sure," Mark said. "But I think I may have known this missing kid." He pointed at the paper.

"I saw it," she said. "That's what scared me

about walking home alone at night. It's awful she's missing, but how could you have known her? How could you know the mayor's daughter?"

"From talking on the Party Line," Mark said.

"I thought you quit after we discussed last month's bill," she said sharply. "You promised, Mark. No more phone bills, you said. I believed you."

"I was going to quit," Mark said. "But before I did I heard a girl named Nicky talking, and I have a feeling this is her."

His mother leaned over and looked at Nicky's picture again. "She's cute," she said. "Her parents must be worried sick."

Yeah, Mark thought. That describes it. Sick. He was glad his mother didn't say anything else about the Party Line. He didn't feel up to discussing his promise to stop calling . . . especially since he hadn't stopped.

Chapter 12

"I'm going to teach you to hurt people," said the instructor. "It doesn't matter how little you are or how big a thug is. If you can gouge out his eye, you'll hurt him. Guaranteed."

Mark looked over at Todd, then at Marcy and Libby. Their expressions mirrored his own surprise and slight feeling of repulsion. This wasn't exactly what we expected, Mark thought.

"My name is Vince," the instructor said. "Hello to anyone who is new, and welcome to 'Fight Dirty and Live.' I'll tell you one thing right off. I'm dead serious. That's why I'm alive. My best friend isn't. There's a coffee can by the door. If you can afford it, put the money in before you leave. If you can't, stay anyway. I need money just like everybody else, but it's more important to me to teach people to survive.

"Thugs have two advantages on you," Vince continued, stalking around the room as if he were looking for victims. He was short and slim, with straight blond hair and a face that never seemed to change expression. "First is surprise. They know they're going to attack you, but you don't know it's coming. Second, they don't care how much they hurt you."

He threw a punch at a girl standing towards the front of the group. She ducked back. He advanced. She screamed. He kept advancing. She leaped at him, her fingers stiffened, going for his eyes.

At the last moment they both stopped, and the girl joined the class again.

"See?" Vince said. "Most of you froze. None of you tried to help her. Part of the reason was you were probably hoping it was a class demonstration. But a big part of the reason was you aren't attackers. It isn't in your nature. We're taught to be nicer than that."

He stood facing the class. He pulled his hair back from his forehead, revealing a jagged scar. "Thugs aren't nice," he said. "They don't care how much they hurt you. But you would probably hesitate to hurt another person, even if he was attacking you. The thought of damaging a living, breathing human being is disgusting to you."

He dropped the hair he'd been holding and let it fall back into place. "I can guarantee you, being a slab of meat on the ground in front of a thug while he attacks your date or kills your child is more disgusting. For you new folks, the first exercise we do every class is imagination and screaming. Sue, will you help me?"

The same girl walked to the front. She pointed at a spot in the air in front of her. "He's attacked four girls," she said. "He thinks I'm going to be next. He's big and fat and gross. He's got a lard-belly and his breath smells. But he's got a knife, too, and he's planning to use it. It's gleaming in the moonlight."

She screamed and leaped at him, digging, kicking, and gouging.

Mark shuddered at the scream and the girl's intensity.

"Think vicious," the instructor ordered. "Think hate. Think damage. You've got a lot of conditioning to overcome before you can defend yourself. This is a warm-up to loosen up your body and loosen up your inhibitions. Go to it."

Mark felt like an idiot until he thought about Nicky. He imagined her, young and trusting. He imagined a man, big and hulking, stalking her. Mark grew angry enough to charge the imaginary thug, kicking and punching.

The instructor blew a whistle and everyone stopped. Mark had been too caught up in the lesson to notice if his friends had done the exercise or not.

"Split up," the teacher said. "New people over here."

Mark, Libby, Todd and Marcy followed the teacher, along with three other people.

He gave them each a flat, evaluating stare. "Kidney," he said. "Eyes. Throat. Nose. Little finger. Groin. Those are the first six places you'll concentrate on."

Vince selected Todd as a model and pointed out the vulnerable spots. "You don't use this stuff in playground fights," he said. "It's not for when you're sparring with friends or arguing with your brothers. This is bloody, painful and gory — it's dirty fighting. There's nothing fair about it, and that's the whole point. There's nothing fair about being attacked, either. Thugs don't follow anybody's rules but their own."

He led them to a corner where people were leaping at black bags with red spots painted on them. The bags were suspended by ropes from hooks in the ceiling. The red marked the six vulnerable spots Vince had listed.

"Divide into teams," he said. "One of you swings the dummy around by manipulating the rope. The other one jumps at the dummy. Go for blood."

He left them, after showing them how to move the dummies. He joined the other groups, one by one.

"Wow!" Libby said. "He's something! He's really intense!"

By the end of class they were all exhausted and sweaty, but full of high spirits.

"I desperately need something," Mark said.

"What?" Marcy asked.

"I'm not sure," Mark said. "Something to eat, and someone to eat it with would be a good start." He lifted his eyebrow in question at Marcy. She nodded.

They dropped their money in the coffee can as they left.

"A good investment," Mark said.

"I hope I never have to use what I learned,"

Marcy said. "But I feel less vulnerable already. In fact, I feel . . . feisty!"

Libby laughed. "It's all that fear," she said. "Mr. Santos would say we're on a natural high."

"Where are we going?" Mark asked. "We passed Todd's car."

"I don't feel like riding," Libby said. "I feel like walking. Or running."

"Me, too," Marcy agreed. "Let's go to After Hours. We can get something to eat there. And we can sit and talk without anyone wishing we'd go someplace else. Besides, it's nearby."

"Sounds good," Todd agreed.

Libby grinned and tapped Todd on the shoulder. "You're IT!" she called. She took off running. Mark and Marcy sprinted after her, with Todd in pursuit.

Chapter 13

Inside After Hours they found a booth along a side wall and ordered ice cream.

Mark studied Marcy while she examined her sundae as if trying to decide where to attack it first. Her dark curls caught the light from the overhead chandeliers so her hair looked like it was shining in the sun. She dug her spoon into the ice cream, swirled the spoon to capture some chocolate syrup and grinned at Mark as she licked the ice cream off.

He wondered what she was thinking and if she was glad she'd gone to the class . . . if she was glad to be with him.

I don't know why she should be, he thought. I'm not exactly a great conversationalist. I did better talking on the Line with Janine. He looked at Todd and Libby, who had discovered a mutual interest in old rock music and were chattering away, absorbed in each other and in their discussion.

Well, at least he's not being shy anymore, Mark thought. Now I'm the one being shy. She probably thinks that means I'm not interested in her. He thought back to his English class, remembering how nervous he'd been when Mr. Santos read his story and how quickly he'd felt more at ease when he realized that everyone had liked it.

But Marcy isn't in my English class, he thought. I don't think I should start talking about blood and guts. Why can't she say something? Can't she tell I don't know what to say? What if she doesn't know what to say, either? It looks like we're in for a very quiet evening!

"Do you have any brothers or sisters?" Marcy finally asked.

Mark shook his head. "Do you?"

"Little ones," she told him. "It's my mom's second marriage. Second family, too. Here I am, almost out of school and she's started all over with kids in diapers. It's crazy."

Once they'd started talking it seemed easier for Mark to think of things to say. "It's like you live in a whole different world from mine," he told her as they all headed back to Todd's car. "I can't imagine having to look where I walk to make sure I'm not going to collide with someone who's shorter than my knees."

"Or having to watch out for Lego people," Marcy said, laughing. "My little brother always has his Legos scattered around everywhere and it hurts his feelings something awful when I step on his Lego friends. He says it kills them. He can't seem to figure out that if he kept them picked up I couldn't kill them."

"Just be glad it isn't frogs," Mark told her. "I collected frogs. One day my mom washed my jeans without checking the pockets, and looking at it now, I'm sure it was better she didn't check. I heard her screaming and ran downstairs to the laundry and there were fourteen of my favorite frogs, dead in the washing machine."

"Oh, yuck!"

"I started screaming then, too," Mark said. "They were my absolute favorite frogs. They looked so pathetic, all clean, of course, but with their little legs all sticking out stiff and their eyes glazed."

"I'd have strangled you!" Marcy said.

"I'm sure Mom wanted to, but I was so upset she couldn't bring herself to even yell at me."

Todd had an arm around Libby, in front of them. They were talking and laughing quietly, Libby's head resting against Todd's shoulder.

Todd unlocked the door to his father's car, a small compact. He held the front seat forward while Mark and Marcy climbed in back. "It's pretty crowded back there," Todd commented. "Sorry. Mom drives a bigger car, but she wanted it tonight. I was lucky to get this one."

"I don't mind," Mark said. "Honest." He was very aware of Marcy's jean-clad knee pressing against him in the cramped backseat. She smelled so good. He wanted the night to go on forever.

Marcy turned slightly, looking up at Mark. "This was fun," she said. "I had a good time."

"I did, too," Mark said. Marcy didn't look away. Mark smiled at her. The lights and shadows played over her face as Todd drove past the streetlights that lined the road. It made her look mysterious and secretive as her face was shadowed, then bright and cheery as the lights shone on her again.

He wished he had enough nerve to kiss her. It would be easy, he told himself. Just lean forward. His heart thudded, but somehow he couldn't make a move. How can something so nice be so scary? he thought.

He sighed. Todd was nearing Marcy's house. Mark could hear Libby's voice in the front seat directing Todd to the third house up past the stop sign.

Coward, Mark told himself. You lost your chance.

He turned towards Marcy to say good night and found she was looking at him thoughtfully. Slowly, she leaned towards him. When their lips met Mark was startled at the softness. Her hair smelled like flowers, fresh and sweet.

"I'll see you at school Monday," she said softly. "At lunch."

"Can't I see you tomorrow?" he asked.

"No," she said. "I can't go out on Sundays. I have to help Mom. House rules."

Libby was spending the night with Marcy. Mark and Todd waited while the girls walked up to Marcy's house, then drove away in silence, lost in their own thoughts.

Mark wondered about his evening, and Marcy. Do I love her? he wondered.

It's too soon to be in love, isn't it?

Yeah, he decided. It's too soon.

Then he remembered his date with Janine in the morning. It would have been awkward if Marcy had said yes to tomorrow! he thought. Two dates at the same time. Somehow, I can't see either Marcy or Janine being very understanding about that!

"That was a close call!" he said aloud.

Chapter 14

Sunday morning Mark caught the bus downtown, staring out the window but not really seeing anything, wondering if he was just being imaginative or if the missing Nicky could really be the girl from the Party Line. He got off at the stop near St. Mark's and climbed onto the low stone wall that surrounded the church, enclosing the neat lawn.

He'd arrived early so he settled down to wait, idly watching the people who passed.

After a while he started thinking about the missing girls again. He didn't notice the tall girl with long, pale brown hair who emerged from the crowd that had crossed the street. He didn't look at her blue sweater, or at the red-and-black checkered jacket she held in her arms.

He didn't see her at all until she stood at his elbow and said, "Mark?"

Then he jumped. He focused on her face. It was clean, free of makeup with naturally pink cheeks, naturally dark eyelashes and eyebrows.

She looked fresh and lovely to Mark, and very much alive.

"Janine?" he asked.

"Are you okay?" she asked. "You look upset."

"Just thinking about a missing girl," he said.

Janine made a face. "The mayor's daughter?" she asked. "There was a segment about her on the news. Did you know her?"

"I think it's our Nicky," he said thoughtfully.

"What do you mean, OUR Nicky?" she asked. "I don't know any Nickys."

Mark looked at her, wondering if she'd think he was crazy if he told her. He decided he didn't care if she did think he was nuts. He had to talk to somebody about it.

"Let's go walk," he suggested. "The park's this way." As they headed up the street he said, "I heard Nicky on the Line. She was talking to oily-voiced Ben. She told him about walking in a field near her house, and listening to the birds sing and seeing animals. And he was trying to get information about exactly where she lived."

"Do you think she told him?" Janine asked.

"She sounded awfully young to me," Mark said. "Even though she said she was fifteen. If she's this Nicky, she was really only thirteen, and it wouldn't be hard to trick a kid into giving more information than she realized she was giving."

Janine frowned.

"I heard her describe herself," Mark went on. "On the Line. If she was telling the truth, it matches the description that was in the paper.

Light brown hair, blue eyes, five-feet-five-inches tall."

"Do you mean you think Ben from the Line kidnapped her?"

"I think somebody did," Mark said. "According to the paper, none of her friends think she ran away, and friends usually know. The problem is, I don't know anything for sure. How can I find out?"

"Oh, Mark," Janine said. "You can't. How could you figure that out? Whoever kidnapped her will send a ransom note and the police will call in the FBI and she'll get saved."

"Or they'll kill her without ever sending a ransom note and I'll feel guilty forever," Mark said. "It seems like I should tell someone what I suspect. If I never say anything and it turns out it was the same guy and he kills her . . . "

They'd reached the park. Janine sat on a bench under a group of graceful red-leaved sumac trees. Mark plunked himself beside her.

"I went to the cops once," Janine said finally. "There was some trouble at home. I thought about it a long time, and I decided the cops would at least look into things if I talked to them."

"And did they?"

Janine made a face. "The courts put me in a foster home for three months," she said. "After three months they sent me back. Nobody did a single other thing — not the courts, the cops or the social workers. Nothing changed except both my parents hate me for interfering and especially for bringing the police in."

She shrugged. "I'm not saying you shouldn't talk to the police, but I am saying they messed up my life royally and didn't do one thing about the problem that I went to them for."

"That isn't very encouraging," Mark said. "But they do have access to more information than I do. I wonder if they could check Nicky's phone bill, and maybe the other girls who've disappeared, too. If they all had calls to the Party Line, maybe the police would take the idea more seriously."

"They might," Janine agreed. "IF they'll bother checking, and IF the girls made the calls from their own homes. They could have made them from someone else's house, so NOT having any calls from the Line on their bills doesn't mean they didn't ever call the Line."

"Yeah," Mark said gloomily. "I don't know what to do. It's silly, but talking with her on the Line makes me feel kind of responsible for her, you know? I feel guilty."

"Why?" Janine asked. "Concerned I can understand, but why guilty?"

"I could have told her to be careful. I thought she sounded awfully young. I could have warned her. I should have warned her."

"Oh, Mark," Janine said. "I talked to her, too. So that makes me as guilty as you are. And I heard her on the Line lots of times, talking to lots of people. Everybody is guilty if anybody is, and IF anything happened. We don't know that anything did. We don't know if this is the same

Nicky. And she could have run away, even if her friends don't think she did."

"Ben was overeager to get personal information from Nicky," Mark said. "I didn't hear all of their conversation, but I heard plenty. I thought he sounded creepy."

"A lot of people are like that on the Line," Janine said. "Everybody on the Line wants to meet someone. That's why they call. I heard Nicky talking to lots of guys, and they all sounded eager. The ones I talk to sound eager. Come to think of it, you did a pretty good job, yourself, convincing me to meet you!"

"I guess you're right," Mark said. "I don't really have anything to go on. But I can't just let it go. I feel like I HAVE to do something."

"Then talk to the cops," Janine said. "Since it was the mayor's daughter maybe they'll be more willing to listen."

Mark was silent for a while, thinking. Maybe it was just his imagination, building something out of nothing.

As he thought, he gradually became more aware of Janine, sitting quietly beside him. He realized they'd been talking like they were old friends. She had a warmth that seemed to touch him, even though they were separated on the bench by several inches. She smelled of soap and ocean breezes.

And she was pretty. Not pretty in a glamorous, perfectionist way, but in an easy, pleasant way that made Mark feel comfortable and unpressured and glad to be with her.

He reached over and took her hand.

She smiled at him.

"You're right about your eyes," he said. "They aren't really green, they're greenish. Next time you describe them, though, you should say something better. Like warm or lively. Or impish. Greenish sounds pretty dull compared to what they really are."

"Impish?" Janine said, breaking into a grin. "I could just hear me saying that! I'd sound like a real weirdo."

"Hey," Mark told her. "I'm glad you gave me a chance. You feel like a friend already. But I'm sorry. I forgot the chipmunk food."

"I've got people food," she said. "We'll share. Let's find a picnic spot."

Janine carried what Mark assumed was an oversized purse or a school bag. She swung it by the strap while they argued over the perfect spot, finally settling on one that was half in the sunshine, half in filtered shade, near enough to the playground to watch the kids playing but far enough away to ignore them if they chose. Then Janine dropped her bag on the table and began pulling out food.

She handed Mark a plastic baggie of sliced fruit, passed him a napkin, pulled out a loaf of French bread, a package of cheese and one of sliced ham, and a baggie of slightly smashed olives. Two cans of grape juice completed the lunch.

"Looks great," Mark said.

"Save some for the chipmunks, remember?" Janine warned.

Mark tore off a hunk of bread and set it aside with a few apple slices. "This enough?" he asked.

He talked easily with Janine while they ate, learning more about her family, asking about friends and school and what she was going to do when she graduated.

"College," Janine said firmly. "I'd like to get completely away from my parents. I can if I go to school out of state. How about you?"

"I don't know," Mark admitted. "Maybe things will suddenly become clear to me before I graduate. My grades aren't good enough for a scholarship, and I'm not sure I want to keep going to school anyway, even if we did have money for college. Which we don't. I guess I'll get a job somewhere and see what happens."

While they were talking Janine made several trails of food by tossing small chunks of bread and apple in a path from some nearby bushes in towards their bench.

"Look!" she whispered, grabbing Mark's arm. She pointed. A little tan nose poked itself out from a cluster of fallen leaves. The nose emerged farther. Then the whole body scurried out. Little paws snatched the piece of apple and then the chipmunk whirled and scuttled back under the leaves.

"He's so cute!" she said.

They fed him for a while and then Janine

started gathering the remains of their lunch. "It's getting kind of late," she said. "I still have homework."

They headed back towards the bus stop.

"I guess I will call the cops," Mark said. "It doesn't seem right not to do anything at all." He took her hand again and they talked about other things for the rest of the walk back to the bus. They exchanged phone numbers. At the bus stop, Mark brushed some pale brown hair back from Janine's face, then kissed her very gently on the lips.

She jerked away, then her face reddened. "I didn't . . . I . . . You startled me!" she stammered.

Mark grinned. "I intend to startle you again," he said. "I'll call you."

She swallowed hard, then looked relieved as her bus hissed to a stop beside her. "Okay," she said. " 'Bye." And she disappeared up the bus steps.

Chapter 15

After school on Monday Mark called the police, asking for the detective in charge of Nicky Youngfield's disappearance.

Detective Laker took the call, sounding tired and impatient.

Carefully, unsure how to phrase it, Mark explained about the Party Line and how he'd heard a girl named Nicky call in, a girl who liked to walk in fields and who had talked with a guy calling himself Ben.

"That's stretching things pretty far, don't you think?" the detective asked.

"Maybe," Mark said.

"Why did they have this private conversation when someone else was on the line with them?"

Mark explained about faking the sign-off tone. There was a long silence when he finished.

"Couldn't you at least check her phone bills?" Mark asked finally. "If she was calling from home it will show up on the bill. That would tell you something."

"Sure. Yeah. We'll do that," Laker said. "Look, son, don't worry. We're working on it around the clock. We'll find her, whether she's a runaway or a victim of foul play. We have the people, and we have the training. We know what we're doing."

Meaning I don't and I should butt out, Mark translated to himself. He hung up, discouraged.

"What did you expect?" Janine asked when he called her. "You're just a dumb kid, right? They're the brilliant cops."

"Maybe we should try something ourselves," Mark said.

"Like what?" Janine asked.

"Listen on the Line. We might hear Ben make arrangements to meet someone else. Then I could go to the same place."

"And do what? Stand on the corner and watch everybody who meets anybody and ask if they're the Party Line people? And then follow them to see if he kidnaps her? Besides, how will you even know he's the one making the arrangements? Will you recognize his voice for sure? What if he doesn't call himself Ben each time?"

"Do you have any other ideas?" Mark asked.

"Yeah, I do. I could call in and talk to guys," Janine said. "I could let the oily-voiced ones talk me into dates and then if somebody tried something funny, we'd know it was him."

"And have you wind up missing, too?" Mark said. "No way, Janine. I don't want the kidnapper anywhere close to you."

"The thought of dates with guys like that doesn't exactly thrill me, either," Janine admitted.

Mark sighed. "Keep thinking," he said.

"Yeah. You too."

Chapter 16

Mark scooped some lasagna into a frying pan and heated it on the stove. He grabbed a fork and ate from the pan. He had just finished running water in it to soak when the phone rang.

"I found a couple of cars," Robbie said.

"Yeah?" Mark's interest in having a car had grown sharply stronger. Aside from the fact that his mother needed one, he thought if he had a car, he might be able to do something about tracking down or following Ben.

"Yeah. One of the women in my class heard I was looking. She said her folks have a couple of cars they've decided to sell. I guess they haven't driven them in a long time."

"When can we go?" Mark asked.

"I told them we'd call," Robbie said. "I wasn't sure when you'd be able to go."

"I can go now," Mark told him. "I want wheels."

Mark met Robbie at his place, and they walked

the six blocks to the address Robbie had gotten
on the phone. The house was in an older section
bordering the blocks of apartments where the
boys lived. The homes there were small and
brick, with wide front porches, and with old trees
and thinning grass out front. There wasn't a tri-
cycle or a swing set to be seen.

They knocked at 217 Holder Place, and
waited. They could hear slow footsteps inside.

The man who finally opened the door was
stooped and gray, with gray hair, gray slacks,
slippers, and a dark blue golf sweater over a pale
gray shirt. It was obvious he had been a big man,
for even with the bent posture of age he was still
as tall as the boys. His face was creased, but his
eyes were bright and aware, his hair newly
trimmed and his handshake firm. "Edward Brindle," he introduced himself.

He led them slowly around the side of the
house along a flagstone path. The garage faced
the alley, and the doors, which were hinged on
the sides like barn doors, were held shut with a
thick padlock.

Brindle unlocked the padlock and swung the
doors open. He flipped on the light.

"Here they be," he said. "I told you they've
been sitting for a spell. Don't know if they'll
start."

"We don't want to start them if they've been
sitting very long," Robbie said.

He and Mark looked at the cars — an old Jeep
wagon and an equally old Chevy sedan. Both cars

squatted low on their saggy tires, seeming to Mark to be silent and hopeful. Mark waited for Robbie to ask the questions.

"Did you drain the oil and the radiator when you stored them?"

Brindle shook his head. "I never actually decided to store them," he said. "I just drove them less and less, and one day I realized it had been a few years since I touched them. Decided I better sell them. No sense letting them sit and grow cobwebs."

"Then for sure we'd better not try to start them," Robbie said, sounding disappointed. "We don't want to spread old oil through the crankcase. We don't want to do anything at all till we've charged up the batteries and checked the wiring and changed all the fluids."

"Well, look them over," Brindle told the boys.

Robbie started over to the Chevy and Mark, relieved, climbed into the Jeep. He'd been hoping for a four-wheel drive for his mother to get to work in the winter, but hadn't figured he had much chance of finding one in their price range. But if there was any hope of getting either of these cars, he wanted the Jeep.

It smelled musty inside, reeking of old oil, mouse droppings and dust. The seats were cracked and foam rubber showed through. There wasn't much else to see. The dash and glove box and all the knobs and switches were in their proper places. He decided the car seemed friendly, though sleepy and unaware. He knew he could wake it up. He knew it would rather be used than sleep out its useful years in an old garage.

He climbed out and opened the hood. He wiggled the hoses and tugged on the belts, opened the radiator and stuck his finger inside, pulled off the distributor cap, then took a look at the wiring, the coil, the starter and the fuel pump.

He looked at the oil stains on the dirt floor of the garage. Without starting the car there wasn't much else he could check.

"How much would you want for them?" Robbie asked.

The old man looked thoughtful.

"Think you could fix these two old guys up all by yourselves?" he asked.

Robbie nodded. "I think so," he said. "I can fix most things on cars, anyway."

"I've had half a dozen people look at these," Brindle said. "The first thing they all wanted to do was fire them up, even though I told them they'd been sitting a long time."

Robbie shuddered. "You didn't let them, did you?" he asked.

"Nope, I didn't. I may be an old man, but I know a few things. And one thing I know is a man's got to respect what a thing's built to do, what its purpose is."

Brindle looked at them slyly. "What I'm saying is, I liked the way you boys respected these cars. You didn't talk about souping them up and wonder how fast they'll go. I liked what you checked and how you checked it. I liked the questions you asked and what you didn't ask. I'm willing to take a chance on you if you're willing to take a chance on me and the cars."

Confused, Mark glanced at Robbie, relieved to see he looked just as confused.

Brindle laughed, as if pleased that he'd out-smarted the boys. "People have been making offers," he said. "Since they always offer low, I've got a pretty good idea what these cars are worth and that's about 800 dollars each."

Mark's hopes fell.

"That's in running condition, though," Brindle said. "I think they'd run if the batteries were just charged up, but I'd rather have them fixed the way they ought to be fixed. So here's my deal. You guys use this garage, but you supply your own tools. You supply the parts. You keep a running list of how much money you put out. I'll call my old garage and get their bid on how much the jobs you do are worth."

I don't see what good that'll do us, Mark thought, his hopes falling even lower. Mom and I could never go 800 dollars.

"And when the cars are running right, we'll take the cost of the jobs and the parts off the 800-dollar figure," Brindle explained. "If we come up with a figure you're willing to pay, the cars are yours for that price. If you're not willing to pay that price, I'll sell the cars to someone who is, but I'll pay you for the parts and labor you put out."

"It sounds like a good deal," Robbie said. "You get the cars fixed and sold either way, and we either get a good deal on a car or a good price for our work."

"So when can you start? Brindle asked.

"You won't gyp us out of the parts, will you?" Mark asked. "I can't afford to buy parts for some-one else's car."

Brindle sighed. "True," he said. "That is a problem. You don't know how honest I am, and I don't know how honest you are. That's why I said we'd be taking a chance on each other."

Mark looked at the Jeep, at Brindle and at Robbie. He looked back at the Jeep. It didn't seem so sleepy now. He moved closer and patted the hood, then glanced up to see Robbie and the old man laughing silently at him, eyes and faces amused. Mark flushed.

"I take it that means yes?" Brindle asked.

Chapter 17

By Thursday Mark had already spent several hours working on the Jeep. He had more work to do yet and Robbie was putting in time every day, but they were hoping to be finished soon.

By Thursday Mark had also made a date with Janine for Friday night and Marcy had made sure he was free after class on Saturday.

In Thursday's paper he'd read an article about another missing girl. She was sixteen. Her name was Terry. Mark thought she looked timid and worried in the newspaper photo.

Thursday again, Mark thought, flopping on the couch after dinner. If I live to be ninety, I'll have lived through 4,680 Thursdays. What on earth does anyone need with that many Thursdays? He stared blankly at the TV, not really watching.

Finally, later Thursday evening, Detective Laker called, still sounding tired and impatient. "There are no Party Line calls on the mayor's phone bill," he said. "Nice try. It was just a co-incidence. But thanks for wanting to help."

"Yeah, sure," Mark said. He jammed the phone back on the hook, tossed his math book aside and stared out the front window, glaring at the people who were walking and driving around outside.

Why weren't there any calls? he asked himself. Did she call from someone else's phone? Was it a different Nicky after all?

Forget it, he told himself. What probably happened was that all the girls just ran away. The Nicky I heard on the Party Line was probably a different Nicky anyway. I guess I was just bored and I let my imagination run wild.

But he couldn't get the missing girls out of his mind. They haunted him while he did his homework and his chores, still bothered him while he tried to sleep. He finally fell asleep with the light on, thinking about them, and then he dreamed.

He dreamed he was watching Nicky from someplace high, someplace too far away to help, even though he could see her as clearly as if she were right in front of him. He watched helplessly as a shadowy figure rose from the weeds and leaped at Nicky, yanking her head back. He heard Nicky's scream of terror, echoing, over and over.

Mark screamed.

He opened his eyes and shut them quickly against the harsh overhead light. He looked around his room, seeing the familiar things as if they were too sharp-edged and not really his. Gradually the horror faded and the room grew more comforting, less alien and hostile.

I'm a little old for this nightmare stuff, he thought. And this business of Nicky is getting a little out of hand. I'm getting a fixation. Maybe I'm obsessed. He finally fell asleep again and this time slept soundly, maybe even dreamlessly, though he was tired in school Friday.

Chapter 18

Being tired didn't stop him from hurrying over to Edward Brindle's garage after school. Robbie was already there.

"I rebuilt the carburetors last night," Robbie announced, peering out from under the Chevy, his hair and shoulders covered with grease. He pointed to some paper bags near Mark's feet. "The antifreeze is in those bags," he said. "Bring them over. Let's get these guys filled up so we can start them."

They poured the fluid into the radiators, added water, and then turned to look at each other, their eyes shining and expectant.

"They're ready!" Robbie said. He reached into the pocket of his coveralls, pulled out two keys and tossed one to Mark. "Let's do it," he said.

He slid onto a cloth he'd spread over the seat of the Chevy and Mark climbed into the Jeep. Grinning, they started the cars. The engines sputtered, echoing raggedly in the garage.

"Quit complaining because I woke you up,"

Mark ordered, patting the dashboard. He revved the engine and when it was warmed up he got out and hooked up Robbie's timing gun. He loosened the distributor and advanced the spark until the engine sounded smooth, then checked the timing marks with the gun. He tightened the distributor and handed the gun to Robbie to use.

Mark stepped back from the Jeep and listened, grinning widely. "It sounds beautiful!" he called. Robbie grinned back.

"Major tune-up, carburetor rebuild, transmission reseal." Brindle's voice came from the open garage doors.

The boys turned to smile at the old man. "Sound nice, don't they?" Robbie asked.

"Pretty," Brindle agreed. "Listen to my list. See if you have anything to add." He went on, listing the work the boys had done that week.

Mark was impressed. He'd put in a lot of time himself, but Robbie had spent several more hours working late into the night. He'd replaced brake shoes, adjusted the clutches and painstakingly checked both cars from end to end.

"I've decided on 400 dollars," Brindle said. "Can you pay that much?" He looked anxious when neither Robbie nor Mark responded.

"I wouldn't sell these cars to anyone else," Brindle said. "Not after all the work you've put in on them. How about 350 dollars each? It wouldn't be right to go any lower, would it? I know they're worth that to you."

"I'll take it!" Mark shouted, stunned. He hadn't actually dared hope the price would be affordable. He'd worked on the Jeep to take his mind off Nicky, to spend time with Robbie and to get some more practical experience. All the time he'd refused to think of the Jeep as his, though he knew he'd already grown attached to it.

Robbie switched both engines off. He didn't say a word to Brindle. He just grinned.

"I already got the titles notarized," Brindle said. "I knew these cars belonged to you guys. Henry down at the corner station does pollution stickers. You'll need them for the new plates."

"Thanks, Mr. Brindle!" Mark said. "I just can't believe it! I have a car! Actually, I guess my mom has a car."

"She's going to let you drive it, isn't she?" Brindle asked.

"Oh, you bet!" Mark said. "Absolutely!"

After Brindle left, Mark and Robbie walked home, making ironic comments about new car owners still being on foot.

"I wish I had the car tonight!" Mark said, thinking of his date with Janine. "I wish we had the plates and stickers and insurance already. We haven't even taken a test-drive."

Robbie gave Mark a knowing look. "Cars make it easier to spend time with girls, don't they," he commented. "You know, you don't sound so confused about them these days."

"About what?" Mark asked. "Girls?" He flushed, remembering his earlier discussions with Robbie about girls. "I just used the information you gave me."

"It must have worked," Robbie said.

"Well, yeah. I just started thinking of girls as people who are just like me, only female. I remember to smile and look them in the eye. It works fine."

"I don't remember saying that," Robbie said.

Oh, Mark thought. That's right. That's what I heard those girls saying on the Party Line. "Well, anyway," he went on. "Whoever said it, it was good advice. It's very simple. Guys want to be with girls, and girls want to be with guys. I've got it all figured out."

Robbie gave him an amused glance. "You'd better write that book," he said.

"What book?"

"The one about understanding girls. Anyone who's an expert owes it to the world to write a book. It's a commonly misunderstood subject."

"I'll be too busy this weekend," Mark said, laughing. "Besides, I'll be even more of an expert by Sunday."

"Why?"

"Well, I have a date tonight with one girl, and a date tomorrow with another one. That should make me an authority by Sunday, don't you think?"

Robbie chuckled. "What I think is you ought to write the book BEFORE this weekend. If you've got two dates, I'd say after this weekend you won't know anything anymore."

"Why?" Mark asked.

"You'll see," Robbie said, still laughing.

Chapter 19

Mark dressed carefully for his date with Janine. He wore his jeans, but chose a tan, long-sleeved shirt with pale blue stripes, and wore a pale blue sweater over it. He combed his hair, wishing he'd gotten it cut so it wouldn't be so curly.

He stared critically at his reflection. I wish my eyes were darker, he thought. Pale blue isn't very exciting. In fact, nothing about me is very exciting. He sighed. Then he grinned.

This isn't exactly your first date with her, he reminded himself. She's already seen you, and you must have looked okay to her because she agreed to go out with you. She must think you're at least okay, and okay is good enough.

The pep talk helped a little, but Mark was still nervous as he caught the bus downtown. He checked again to be sure he had his wallet, and when he got off the bus, shivering in the blast of cold air, he shrugged on his old blue jacket even though he'd decided earlier that he looked better with it off.

Janine was perched on the low stone wall in front of St. Mark's, waiting. She waved when she saw him. She had on jeans, too, and her black-and-red checkered jacket with a black knit scarf wrapped around her neck.

"Hi!" she called.

Mark stopped right in front of her, staring intently. Her cheeks were reddened from the cold, her greenish eyes lit with what looked to Mark like mischief.

She reddened even more under his scrutiny.

"Why are you staring at me?" she asked.

"I'm memorizing you," Mark said. "When I got home after the last time I realized I could remember all the things you said and did but when it came to what you looked like, all I could think of was the description of yourself you gave on the Line. So I'm making up for that now."

"Well, quit, okay?" she said. "You're making me nervous, just staring like that."

"Then we're even," Mark told her. "I'm nervous, too, from wondering whether you'll like me or not."

"I already do," she said. "Why do you think I agreed to see you again?"

"That's what I kept telling myself," Mark said. "But I was still nervous."

"I am freezing to death," Janine told him. "Could we walk or something?"

"Yeah, let's." Mark offered his hand and Janine took it, hopping down from the wall. "What do you want to do tonight?" he asked.

"Something warm," Janine said. "I know, let's go to the zoo!"

"That isn't very warm," Mark said doubtfully. "Is it open?"

"It's open till nine," she told him. "And it's warm inside the exhibits. The birds are inside, and so are the pachyderms, the monkeys, the giraffes, the camels and the lions."

"I haven't been to a zoo since I was about five years old."

"Then it's time to go again," she said.

"I'll trust you," Mark said. "If you were a kidnapper, you'd have nabbed me already."

"Napped," Janine corrected. "Kidnappers nap their prey, kidnabbers nab." She looked at him, frowning thoughtfully. "If I was going to nap somebody I guess it would be you. It would definitely have to be someone about your height, with light blue eyes just like yours, and with kind of curly brown hair, just about like yours. So I guess you would do."

She likes my hair, Mark thought, feeling better about the haircut he hadn't gotten.

"And what else?" he asked.

Janine laughed. "You're greedy!" she said.

"There's something you should understand," Mark told her. "Flattery will get you anywhere."

"Ah, but where do I want to go?" Janine asked.

"To the zoo. Did you forget already?" Mark was pleased at how easily Janine manipulated their conversation, how quickly she answered back to his comments, how she could jump from teasing to laughter to seriousness and back again.

"I'd nap an elephant," Janine said. "But they're stubborn. They also don't like riding on buses, so they're hard to take places."

"Maybe you should stick with napping me," Mark suggested.

"Elephants are cuddlier," Janine said.

"They are not!" Mark protested. Cold air swirled around them and they hurried to zip their jackets as they ran for the bus stop. "I'm cuddlier than any elephant you've ever cuddled," Mark said. "And I'll prove it, too."

"Okay," Janine told him. "I dare you to prove it."

They caught the bus at the corner and sat together in the very back. Mark put his arm around Janine, still holding her other hand.

"How am I doing?" he asked after a while.

"I don't have enough evidence," Janine said. "I can't decide without more evidence. I want to be fair about this."

Mark gently turned her face up towards his. . . .

"Zoo!" the bus driver called.

They jumped and pulled apart, Janine's eyes laughing though her facial expression was pretend-serious.

"It's the elephant's turn, now," she said.

They wandered, holding hands and eating popcorn. They admired the animals when they remembered to, but spent more time looking into each other's eyes than watching the zoo creatures.

"It's almost nine," Janine told him finally. "We've got to go if we're going to catch the bus. It's the last one from here."

"I hadn't thought about getting home," Mark admitted. "But the buses don't run very late, do they? I don't want you to go home yet."

Janine led the way through the turnstiles and down to the bus stop. "I don't have a whole lot of choice," she said. "This is the last bus from the zoo home. I've got to be on it if I want to get home without walking. You'll have the car licensed and inspected and all pretty soon, right? We can handle an early date this one time."

Mark dropped the fare in the box and followed Janine to the back of the bus again. "Isn't there somewhere within walking distance of your place where we could go for a while?" he asked. "We could go dancing or sit and talk and I'd walk you home later."

"Then how would you get home?" she asked.

"Walk or hitch."

"That sounds scary to me," Janine said. "And dangerous."

"It just seems so early to me," Mark said. "I'm not ready to end my evening. I still want to spend it with you."

"My folks are gone," Janine said slowly. "You can come over for a while."

Though no one had pulled the cord, the bus stopped.

"You getting off?" the driver called.

"Yeah," Janine said. "Thanks, Ed."

Mark looked at her, startled. Janine smothered a giggle and headed for the steps. She waved as the driver pulled away.

"Ed?" Mark said.

"I ride the buses a lot," she said. "I know a lot of the drivers. Come on. I don't want to stand around in the cold."

Chapter 20

Janine set off briskly and Mark grabbed her hand. Her house was one long block from the bus stop, a large, modern-looking house with a separate four-car garage, a huge front lawn lit by spotlights, and a boat draped in canvas parked alongside the garage. Mark stared in awe.

"You never told me you were rich," Mark said.

"I'm not. It's called successful," she said bitterly. "And it's what my folks are, not what I am. Now you know why the cops didn't believe me that time. Successful families don't have problems, you see." She strode angrily up the sidewalk and unlocked the front door.

Mark followed her inside, into a redwood and plant-filled entry hall the size of his apartment living room. She led him into the kitchen, which was decorated in brick-red and gray, with splashes of bright green provided by plants and by the accent pieces — towels, canisters, picture frames. Mark had never seen a decorated kitchen before.

"This is incredible," he said finally. "Do you know how to use this kitchen?"

"Sure," Janine said shortly. "Does that mean you're hungry?"

"I'm always hungry," Mark said. "But I was curious, too. I don't even know what some of this stuff is, much less how to use it."

Janine yanked open the fridge and rummaged through the containers on the shelf. She chose three, slapping them on the counter.

"Hey," Mark said. "I didn't mean to make you mad. What did I say? We don't have to eat if you don't want to."

Janine took a deep breath and let it out slowly. "I'm not mad at you," she said. "It's this place. I hate it. I hate how impressed people always are when they come here. They think it's SO fabulous and I'm SO lucky to live in a place like this and I must be SO happy. But if you ask me, this place is full of rotten people and I don't think I'm lucky at all to be stuck here with rotten people. It stinks!"

"Hey, hey," Mark said. He took her hand, feeling clumsy. "I'm sorry I was impressed," he said. "I'll hate it too if you want. Would that help?"

Janine giggled.

Startled, Mark leaned back to look at her face.

"You'll hate it?" Janine teased, shaking her head at him. "What kind of thing is that to say? You don't have any reason to hate it — you'll just do it? Just like that? It can't be a very high quality hatred if you can turn it on and off on demand. Would you hate anything I wanted you to?"

"Sure," Mark agreed.

"How about this harmless little button?" she asked, touching a button on Mark's shirt.

"I hate it," he said solemnly.

Janine giggled again. Mark grinned, then laughed. Janine laughed, too, the laughter releasing her anger and tension. She put the first plastic container in the microwave oven, programming it quickly. Mark watched.

"I've never seen one cook before," he admitted.

"It's not very interesting to look at," Janine said, stooping to peer through the glass-fronted door with him. "But it's fun to use." She pulled the first container out when the oven dinged. Then she put the second one in. She tapped the touchpad numbers quickly and the oven hummed into action.

When the last container was finished Janine grabbed two cans of diet Coke and a handful of napkins. "You get those," she directed, nodding towards the counter. "Then follow me. I'm taking you to my hideaway. You're being napped."

Mark stacked the containers and lifted them. "Okay," he said.

Janine glanced back over her shoulder. "You're being awfully agreeable about being kidnapped," she said.

"I always am when my napper is such a sweet, lovely young thing," Mark said.

"Woman, not thing," Janine corrected.

"Right."

"Quit leering," she said. "You're much too

young to leer. You don't look evil enough, either. You've got to have the right kind of face and personality to leer successfully, and you just don't have them."

Mark followed her through the kitchen into an entertainment room with an enormous stereo system, racks of tapes and records, a VCR set-up and a pool table. He glanced appreciatively at everything but didn't mention anything.

Janine opened a door. Behind it was a set of stairs leading down, and a ladder, leading up. She climbed up. Mark followed. They ended up in a loftlike room, equipped with huge pillows and a telephone, a bookshelf, a very small refrigerator and an old chest.

"My hideaway," Janine said. She slid a panel, showing Mark the view down into the entertainment room, then pulled aside some curtains revealing a view into a tree.

"I can climb the tree and then climb in here through the window," Janine said. "If the window's open, anyway. Maybe some day I'll leave it open for you to climb in."

"Just let me know," Mark said. "I was quite a climber in my younger days. Is this where you call the Party Line from?"

She nodded. "This is my place," she said. "It's just about the only place in this house that I like. No one else ever comes here. Sometimes I wonder if my folks even remember it's here."

She arranged the plastic containers on napkins, handed Mark a Coke and spread the rest of the napkins out on the carpet. She opened the food.

"Dim sum," she said. "That's our appetizer. And fried rice. I forget what this is called but it's deep-fried pork in sweet-and-sour sauce. The cook is on a Chinese kick this month."

"Smells great," Mark said. "But what do we eat it with?"

Janine scooped some fried rice up with her fingers. She grinned as she ate it from her hand. "You think nappers provide you with china and silver?" she asked. "What do you think all the napkins are for?"

"To go with the napper, I guess," Mark said. He dug in with his fingers, feeding himself, and sometimes Janine. When the food was gone and they'd cleaned themselves satisfactorily with the napkins, Mark set the containers and the trash aside. He scooted close to Janine. He smiled, looking into her eyes.

"I love nappers with greenish eyes and dumb brown hair," he said. He felt his heartbeat speed up and excitement made his knee joints tingle. That must be what weak-kneed means, he thought absently.

The loft's soft lamplight fell over his shoulder onto Janine's face. Somehow, with her he felt only a little of the shyness he'd felt with Marcy. He kept smiling, watching her face. Slowly her eyes softened, losing the worried lines. She smiled back.

He kissed her.

His heartbeat thudded loudly in his ears. Janine's arms tightened around him and her breath came faster, too. Then she broke loose, panting. Her eyes were huge and shocked.

Mark took a deep breath and let it out slowly. "Wow!" he said, grinning at her. "If we could harness that, we'd be rich."

She sat up, out of his reach.

"Say something," Mark pleaded. "I'm beginning to feel like I did something wrong."

"Almost," Janine said softly. After a pause, she said, "I never felt like that before. It was kind of scary, you know?"

Mark nodded. "I know," he said. "I felt it, too. My heart's going a mile a minute."

"I see now why people get themselves into trouble," Janine said soberly. "I thought kissing was kind of boring before. I didn't understand. I didn't know it could be like that."

Mark rolled up onto his knees and knee-walked over to her. She didn't retreat, but she didn't move towards him, either. Her eyes still looked startled, and a little frightened.

Mark put his arms around her, just holding her. "All you have to do, ever, is say no," he whispered. "That's all. But I don't want to stop kissing you now."

"Just kissing?" Janine asked.

"And holding," Mark said. "That's all."

He kept his word, marveling later at how quickly the following hours had passed. It was nearly one A.M. when Janine finally, reluctantly, sent him home, her cheeks pink and her eyes sparkling, her hair rumpled and her lips curved in a secretive smile.

He thought about her as he walked in the crisp October night, his thumb held out whenever a car drew near. He thought about her through his two rides, one from a suit-clad businessman who dropped him off near the highway, one from a car full of young women going home from working the second shift at the electronics factory where they assembled solid-state circuitry. They dropped him about a mile from his apartment, waved and drove on.

I think I'm in love, Mark decided, grinning happily. He still felt the warmth of Janine's arms, felt it all through the chilly walk, felt it as he climbed into bed, still smiling.

Chapter 21

Saturday afternoon the weather turned colder, with low clouds and sprinkles of rain. Mark hurried to the self-defense class, joining Todd, Marcy and Libby just as class started.

"You'd have to study martial arts for years to be truly confident facing an attacker," Vince said. "Especially an armed attacker. The best advice is to avoid armed attackers."

The class laughed, and Vince nodded. "I see you got my point. It isn't always possible to avoid the unpleasant things in life."

As he had the week before, Vince called the new people to him after the screaming and leaping warmups that loosened both bodies and inhibitions.

The next exercise took place in a darkened corner where a movie projector showed a film of a man armed with a knife and later with a gun. The image was projected life-sized onto a thick mat that hung against the wall.

"This is a little more lifelike than the bags,"

Vince told them. "Don't let it bother you that your attacker never seems affected by anything you do. Take turns and smash him."

The filmed thug lunged, aimed his weapon, grabbed, dodged, threatened, over and over again. Mark figured out that the movie was on a continuous reel, repeating itself endlessly while students bashed at the image. Slowly he got involved in the exercise, forgot the mat, the projector, forgot that he couldn't damage the thug no matter what he did. He attacked, going for the vulnerable spots, going for blood.

When his turn ended he watched the others. He saw when they reached the point of forgetting, too, and began to take the drill seriously.

At the end of the class, Vince had a few closing comments. "Heads bleed easily," he said. "Blood in the eyes stings and blinds a person. Keep your own head safe, and go for the attacker's head. If you can blind him, you have a better chance of escaping."

"Why is the little finger one of the vulnerable spots?" Mark asked.

"The finger bones are small and sensitive," Vince said. "The hands are specially designed to feel and they're easier to hurt than an arm or leg is. If you whack an attacker's hand he'll have a harder time using it to hurt you with, or to hold a weapon with. But there's another reason. Let me show you a very painful grip. It works best on the little finger, though you can use it on any finger. It crimps a nerve."

Vince made his left hand into a loose fist, palm

up. He lined the fingertips of his right hand up against the blunt edge of the other hand, his right index fingertip against the back, bottom knuckle of the left pinky.

"Take the tip of your right thumb," he directed them. "Place it against the nail of your left pinky. See how you've captured the left pinky? Now pinch with your thumb, pushing the nail of the pinky backward towards your index finger and upward at the same time. But not too hard or you'll hurt yourself. It's a good way to convince someone to let go of you!"

Mark tried it and yelped in pain. Marcy laughed at him.

"Now I know what to do if you get too grabby," she said.

"Try telling me to let go, first, okay?" Mark said. "That really hurts!"

The four friends dropped their money into the coffee can and debated how to spend their evening. Todd hadn't been able to get a car so they were on foot until eleven, which was the latest time Libby's mother would agree to pick up the girls.

"I don't want to walk too far in this rain," Libby said. "Anyway, Mom's picking us up at Big Al's. I didn't know where to tell her, so I picked an ice-cream parlor. It seemed like a good place."

"I've never heard of it," Mark said.

"It's by the roller rink," Todd told him.

"That's helps a lot," Mark said. "I never heard of a roller rink around here, either."

The girls exchanged secretive, amused glances. Mark looked from Libby to Marcy. Their eyes had brightened with the same thought, whatever it was.

"What's up?" Mark asked suspiciously. "You two are hatching something. I can tell."

Libby grinned. "No we're not," she denied. "We were remembering something. We used to go skating in junior high. Dim lights, music, holding hands with guys and drifting around the room. It was romantic."

"Let's do it!" Marcy suggested. "Please?"

"I can't skate," Todd said.

"I can," Mark said. "At least I used to be able to. It's been a long time. I don't know if I could do it now."

"Are you game or not?" Libby asked Todd. She made it a dare or a challenge; Mark wasn't quite sure which.

Todd scowled, then he shrugged. "I guess so," he said.

Mark grinned at Marcy and she blushed.

The blush made her cheeks pink and made her eyes sparkle again. Mark found it difficult to look away from her.

Then he remembered the other pink cheeks and bright eyes, from last night. Janine.

Marcy smiled and his heart lurched. He reached over and took her hand.

Oh, Janine, he thought. Oh, Marcy. Oh my.

They laughed and talked during the walk to the roller rink. It only took Mark a few minutes to get used to being on skates again and he and

Marcy held hands, skating around to the music and laughing at Todd, who was gripping the side-rails in white-knuckled desperation, trying not to fall.

"Now show me the nicest, most private, darkest, most romantic corner," Mark said.

"Can't," Marcy said. "I just saw Todd and Libby heading that way."

"Where's the second-best corner, then?" he asked.

Grinning shyly, Marcy skated off and Mark followed, grabbing her around the waist when she stopped. He skated her back into the corner and they sank down onto the small, round, carpeted skate-changing seat.

When Todd and Libby interrupted them, Mark was shocked to learn that it was after ten. He knelt down to help pull Marcy's skates off, noticing that she looked as flushed as Janine had, with the same secretive smile. He felt a pang of guilt, which confused him. Why should I feel guilty? he asked himself. I haven't done anything wrong.

The rain had stopped and the night seemed warmer. At first they laughed at how odd it felt to be walking again, but then Marcy fell silent.

"What's the matter?" Mark asked softly. He had his arm around her shoulder and he pulled her a little closer.

Marcy shook her head, looking down at the sidewalk. Finally she sighed. "I'd like to know . . . I mean, do you like me?" she asked.

"Of course!" Mark said, startled. "Couldn't you tell?"

"I could tell something," Marcy said, glancing quickly at him. Her eyes returned to the pavement. "But I'm not sure what. I mean . . . "

She stopped, seeming reluctant or confused. Mark waited for her to continue. When she didn't, he said, "Marcy, what are you asking me? I feel really stupid, but I don't know what's going on."

"Am I your girlfriend?" she whispered.

"Of course," Mark said.

She smiled at him happily, then looked at the sidewalk again. "Are we going together?" she asked.

"Do you mean like going steady?" Mark asked, feeling suddenly alarmed as he figured out what was bothering Marcy.

"Yeah." It was a whispered answer, but Mark heard it clearly.

"Oh, Marcy," he said. He didn't know what to say after that. And since Marcy's silence seemed to grow deeper, he knew he hadn't said the right thing at all. He suddenly remembered Robbie's wry grin when they talked about the book Mark was going to write. Understanding girls.

Now I know why he told me to write it before this weekend and not after, Mark thought glumly.

Marcy shrugged out from under his arm, moving away from him.

I really blew it, Mark thought. He took ahold

of Marcy's arm, turning her to face him. Ahead of them, Todd and Libby paused in front of Big Al's, looked back, then waved and went inside.

"Look, Marcy," Mark said. "I'm new at this. I never really dated anyone before you, and I never really kissed anyone, either."

Marcy glanced at him quickly, surprised.

"I like you a lot," Mark went on. "I love spending time with you. You're fun. You're nice to be around. You're cute. I hope we keep on dating for a long time."

Marcy gave him a shy, tentative smile.

Mark grinned back.

"But?" Marcy said. "I know there's a but in there somewhere."

Mark's smile faded. "I'm seventeen," he said. "You're my first girlfriend. But I have a second girlfriend, too."

"Fast worker," Marcy commented, her voice shaky.

"I made a date with her before we went out the first time," Mark said. "And I like her a lot. She's very nice. You are, too. Having two special girls in my life is the most wonderful thing that ever happened to me. It's also the most confusing. I LIKE you. Both of you. Is that so awful? Is it?"

Marcy raised her eyes to his. "You really, really like me?" she asked.

"Really, really," Mark said.

"But not enough to go steady?"

Mark sighed. "I like you that much," he said.

"But how could we go steady? That wouldn't be fair."

"To her."

"To all of us," Mark said. He put his arms around her again, cradling her to him in spite of her stiff resistance. "Do you see what I'm saying?" he asked. "Does it make sense?"

Marcy sighed. "I wanted to be special to you," she said.

"Why can't you believe that you are special to me?"

"Do you kiss her like that, too?"

Oh, help! Mark thought. What do I say now? How did I get myself into this mess? Instead of saying anything he tried to kiss Marcy. She turned her head away, but Mark kissed her neck, her cheek. Finally he felt her give in, felt it in the way she relaxed in his arms. She turned her head towards him, only a little, but it was enough.

Mark made it a very gentle kiss until he was sure she wouldn't pull away from him, then he put more feeling into it.

When they finished, what she said again was, "Do you kiss her like that, too?"

Mark dropped his arms. "If she asked me a question like that about you would you want me to answer it?" he asked.

"Of course not!" she said. "What we do is our business, not . . . Oh. I see."

Mark sighed. "This is very confusing," he told her. "But we are way too young to push everybody else out of our lives. When are you going to get married?"

Marcy looked startled. "Some day," she said. "Certainly not for a long time."

"Why not?" Mark asked.

"And miss everything?" Marcy said, sounding horrified. "I want to go to the prom and finish school. I want to get an apartment with my girlfriends and get a job. I want to go to college and live in a dorm. I want to do a ton of things before I settle down and get married!"

Mark grinned. After a while Marcy smiled back. "Okay, I get your point," she said. "Even though going steady is a whole lot different from getting married! Does she go to our school?"

"No."

"Good. Can I count on dates to the school dances, then?"

Mark's thoughts flashed to Janine. Would she want to go to dances at his school with him? He didn't know, but he thought it would be nice to take her. Of course, then Marcy would be there, too. Maybe that wasn't such a good idea.

As if she had read his mind, Marcy sighed. "To SOME of them?"

"Absolutely," Mark said.

"I guess that means you're still going to flirt in the halls, too," she said.

Mark blinked in surprise. "Do I?" he asked.

"All the time," Marcy said. "You're always looking at girls and smiling."

"I thought I was just being friendly," Mark said.

"Being that friendly with girls is flirting," Marcy said firmly. "And you flirt a lot."

If I notice girls, I'm flirting! Mark thought. If I don't, I'm being unfriendly and I hurt their feelings. I can't win. He sighed and walked into Big Al's with Marcy.

Since it was almost time for Libby's mother to pick up the girls, Mark and Marcy only ordered small cones. While she licked her cone Marcy gave him thoughtful, frowning looks. After a while, she smiled.

Mark wasn't sure what had been going on in Marcy's mind, but he decided a smile was a good sign. He also decided he was never going to understand girls. He sighed again. Looks like I'm never going to get that book written! he thought.

Chapter 22

Late Monday afternoon, Mark drove down the highway in the Jeep, retracing his journey from Janine's house. He hadn't paid much attention to the route Friday night, but he had an unfailing sense of direction, as he'd told Janine on the phone earlier. He'd refused her offer of directions, insisting that he and the Jeep could make it to her house without help.

When he'd gotten home from school he'd found a note from his mother along with an envelope and a check for $350.00, signed and made out to Edward Brindle. The note said she'd arranged for insurance but would need the VIN number and the information from the title so would he please leave it out for her tonight. The cash, she explained, was for license plates and gas.

In the envelope Mark had found a fifty-dollar bill, two twenties and a ten. He'd taken the check and the cash and hurried over to Brindle's house. As he hoped, Robbie was there. Robbie had already taken care of the official details for his car and was screwing his new license plates onto the Chevy.

"I'm street legal, now," Robbie had said. "I'll take you to get your plates if you like."

Mark had grinned. "I was hoping you would," he'd admitted. "I don't know where to go."

"Hey, Mark," Robbie had said. "You know my class? The auto mechanics class? I was thinking while we worked on these cars. You interested in being an assistant?"

"Me?"

"Sure. I know you can do tune-ups. And hoses and belts, too, right?"

"Sure I can DO them, but I don't know if I can teach someone else to do them."

"All you have to do is hold up a wrench and a plug and demonstrate how to use them," Robbie had said.

"It sounds easy."

"It is. You wouldn't get paid much, but it would be something. And I could use the help."

"Sounds great," Mark had told him.

With only two wrong turns, Mark found Janine's house. She was waiting for him on the lawn, which was still green and lush though the October nights had been chilly enough to turn all the flowerbeds brown and scraggly. Janine admired the car, walking all the way around it, telling Mark to open the hood so she could see inside.

"What's his name?" she asked.

"It's a Jeep," Mark said. "A Quadra-Trak Wagoneer."

"Jeep is the manufacturer," Janine said. "I want to know the car's name. Your name is Mark. What's his name?"

"I hadn't thought about a name," Mark said.

"Poor, unnamed little thing," Janine said, patting the car. "He'll tell you, if you listen," she told Mark. "Pay attention." She climbed in and fastened her seat belt. "Okay," she said. "Go."

"Where?"

"Wherever he wants," Janine said. "He wants to show off. So let him."

"I'd think you were strange," Mark said, starting the car, "except that you're right. That's exactly what he wants to do."

He pulled away from the curb, driving wherever the car aimed them. He turned onto the highway, off again, drove up hills on dirt paths and through neighborhoods on neatly paved roads.

"Do you want the radio on?" Mark asked. "It works."

"Not yet," Janine said. "I'm still listening to the car." She leaned back in the seat, eyes closed, enjoying the smooth drone of the engine and the other noises the Jeep made bouncing over ruts and through small gullies and potholes on the dirt roads.

Eventually Janine opened her eyes. "He's a nice little car," she said.

"Little?" Mark asked. "This is about the maximum size a car can get and still be a car."

"What did you say?" Janine asked, sounding excited.

"I said, this is about the maximum — "

"Stop right there," she said. "I think you just named your car."

"Maximum?" Mark asked doubtfully.

Janine giggled. "Not Maximum," she said. "Max. His name is Max."

"Not bad!" Mark said. "Max it is."

She flipped the radio on, searching until she found a station she liked.

"Go ahead and set the button," Mark told her.

She set that station and found two others she liked, setting them, too. A song ended and the disk jockey gave the weather report, then moved on to the news. He went through the world news, the major state news, then, his voice dropping a little, but still in the clipped, matter-of-fact manner in which he'd delivered the rest of the news, said, "The mystery of the missing girls continues. Another teenager, Susan Lynne Blakely, has been reported missing by her parents, Mr. and Mrs. George A. Blakely. Their daughter was last seen two days ago when she left for her music lesson. She never showed up for the lesson. She is described as slim, dark-haired, about five-feet-six inches tall and was last seen wearing a plaid skirt and red sweater. Anyone who might have information about her is asked to call the police department. In other news — "

Janine turned the radio off. "Not again!" she said. "What's going on in this town?"

Mark pulled to the side of the road and stopped

the car. "Janine, do you think those girls are running away?" he asked.

"I can't even guess," Janine said. "Kids do run away, but this seems like an awful lot of runaways all of a sudden."

"Have you thought any more about calling the Line?" Mark asked.

"It isn't necessarily one of those guys," Janine.

"I know," Mark said. "But what if it is? It might be Ben. It might be Robert or one of the other oily guys. There seem to be several of them. It might not be anyone from the Line at all. But we'll never know unless we do something to find out."

"What will I do once I get ahold of them?" Janine asked.

"Meet them. One at a time."

"Where? Where is somewhere safe enough?"

"The zoo?" he suggested. "It's too public for him to do anything. You can meet him somewhere specific, so I can already be there, waiting."

"It might work," Janine said slowly. "But once we've seen him, then what? How will we know if it's him? How will we know if he's a kidnapper?"

"I don't know," Mark admitted. "All I have is a plan for meeting him in the first place. I don't know what we'll do after that. I don't even know why I want to do that much, except that if someone is using the Party Line to meet girls and kidnap them, I want him stopped. Maybe once we've met these guys we can tell if they're creepy or weird. Maybe that will give us an idea what to do next. I've got a car now. Maybe we can follow them. We can see where they live, see if they're married, see something, anyway. I just feel like I have to do something. That's all."

Mark massaged his neck with his fingertips. "It's like having a suspicion makes me responsible for the girls, somehow. I'm glad you understand." He remembered thinking he was obsessed about Nicky. Maybe I am, he decided. But Janine will help. We can be obsessed together. "It might be dangerous," he told her. "Are you sure you want to get involved?"

"Can YOU drop it?" Janine asked. "Can YOU just forget it?"

Mark looked at her. "No," he said. "I can't."

"Neither can I," she said. "So what choice do we have? You tried the police and didn't get anywhere. What else is left but for us to do something?"

"Okay," Mark said reluctantly. "Just promise me you won't let anybody get his hands on you. And that you won't go anywhere with any of them."

Janine promised. She scooted across the seat and hugged Mark.

After he dropped Janine off, Mark drove around for a while thinking. Then he headed for home. As he climbed the steps to the lobby, he was still thinking. Nicky . . . Susan . . . so many girls were missing. When would it end?

Mark opened the door of the apartment, stopping short at the angry glare from his mother. She was standing in the living room, holding a yellowish envelope in one hand, tapping it against the palm of her other hand.

Uh-oh, Mark thought.

Chapter 23

"Do you know what this is?" she asked.

"Phone bill?" Mark guessed.

"A ninety-two-dollar phone bill," she replied, handing it to him. "The ninety-two dollars is all Party Line calls. In one month!"

"Before you blow up, can I say a few things?" Mark asked.

She took a deep breath and released it slowly. "I'm counting to ten," she said. Then she nodded. "Go ahead. Say your piece."

Mark tossed his books onto the couch, followed by his jacket. "I got a job," he said. "I'll pay the bill. That's the first point."

"Okay," she said. "I'm still listening."

Mark thought for a moment. He had something to say but wasn't sure how to say it. "I'm sorry about the money," he said finally. "But it wasn't wasted, honest. I needed to make those calls. I needed to have people to talk to. I don't anymore."

She glanced sharply at him, not convinced.

"I know I said last month that I wouldn't make any more calls," he told her. "And then I made even more. I tried not to, but I had to. I've met a nice girl, though — on the Line as a matter of fact—and I have her home phone number now. But there's more to it than that."

He frowned, thinking again. "I haven't called in a couple of weeks," he said. "I haven't wanted to. I haven't even thought about calling and I don't miss it at all. I don't care about it anymore. Does that make sense?"

She sighed. "I guess, in a way. You've outgrown it?"

"Yeah. Maybe that's it. For a while there I felt like I was all alone. You worked all the time, my friends weren't available, Dad was so far away. I didn't have anything I wanted to do, and nobody to do it with anyway. So I used the Line to get involved."

"I don't see how talking to strangers helped you get involved," she said.

"I know. It's kind of weird," Mark agreed. "And what's funny is I didn't even talk that much. I listened. I guess hearing other people's problems helped me put up with my own better, somehow. Anyway, it's finished. I don't have any impulse to call at all anymore. So there won't be any more bills. Okay?"

She nodded. "Okay. Tell me about your job."

They moved into the kitchen so Mark could make a snack. He made himself a pair of peanut butter sandwiches and told her about Robbie's job offer. "Looks like I'll be teaching Saturdays," he said. "Can I have the car Saturday night?"

"The car!" she said. "I'd like to see my car, if you don't mind. I've paid for it, but I haven't seen it yet."

Mark led her outside and around the corner to the dirt lot the residents used as a parking lot. He was eager for his mother to like the car as much as he did, but even so, giving her the keys was difficult. He didn't want to give them up, not even to the person who actually owned the car.

"Well?" Mark asked. "What do you think?"

His mother smiled. "It's wonderful!" she said. "I'm going to love it. Thank you for all the work you put into it."

Mark swallowed hard, keeping his protest inside. It's her car, he reminded himself. He couldn't help feeling depressed, though, as if he'd lost a friend.

" 'Bye, Max," he said aloud.

"What?"

"Max," he repeated. "The car's name is Max."

To his surprise, his mother nodded thoughtfully. "Max fits him just fine," she said. "Max it is."

Back upstairs she made a small pot of decaffeinated coffee, and she and Mark sat at the table with cups, blowing on the coffee to cool it faster.

Mark looked at the clock. "You're not at work!" he said.

She grinned. "I thought you'd never notice," she said. "I got a new job. Miss Typist of the senior class will be doing data processing for the phone company — working real hours. Nine to five. Just like a real person. No more walking home late at night."

"That's great!" Mark told her.

"Anyway," she said. "Steps number one and two have been accomplished. New car. New job. I'm not stopping now. I promised myself I'd keep making changes until things are the way I want them to be. That means meeting men, dating, and all that stuff. I'm a little scared. Starting over isn't all that easy."

"Speaking of dating," Mark said, "can I have the car Friday and Saturday night?"

"Actually," his mother said, "I have a date. Both nights."

"Already?" Mark asked.

"His name is John. Friday night he's taking me out to dinner, so you can have the car. But Saturday I'll need it to meet him. There's a show we want to see, and he doesn't get off early enough to pick me up and still make the show. We won't need Max once I get there, though. You could drive me over there, I guess, and then take the car."

"But I'll be at the rec center," Mark said.

"Oh. Well."

"Maybe my friends and I could all walk over after the self-defense class and get the car."

"I'll be leaving it at the gas station over by Scotty's pizza place," she said. "It's not that close to the rec center."

"That's okay, forget it," Mark said. "Only maybe John could pick you up next time?"

She laughed. "We did without a car all this

time," she said. "And now one isn't enough." She gave him a glance that was half-amused and half-disgusted. "I was all set to have a fit about the phone bill, you know," she said. "And ground you and take away your car keys and everything. You sure talked yourself out of trouble that time!"

"Thank goodness!" Mark said, stuffing the last of the sandwiches into his mouth.

When the phone rang he swallowed hastily and answered. It was Janine.

"All set," she said. "I got Ben on the Line. I'm sure it was Ben, even though he said his name was Richard. But he sounded as oily as Ben, the way you described him. There can't be two of them that bad. So I set it up. For Friday night. He didn't like my arrangements. He kept suggesting other places to meet, but I said it was the zoo or nothing so he finally agreed."

"Did you set up where you'd meet him?" Mark asked.

"Yeah. I said I'd meet him at five-thirty at the bench in front of the penguins. You'll be on the lawn behind them, right? I'll panic if you're not there."

"We're going together," Mark said. "I'll have the car so I'll pick you up. Let's plan on getting there early, before five, even, just in case he comes early, too."

They made the arrangements and Mark hung up, worried. He didn't like using Janine as bait, didn't like being involved with a man who might be a kidnapper. It seemed dangerous, but he couldn't think of anything else to do.

He did his homework, though when he'd finished he couldn't remember a thing he'd just done. He went to bed feeling like he'd slipped into something too deep to get out of and too slippery to hold onto.

Friday morning he met Marcy at her locker. "Are we still going out after class Saturday?" he asked.

Marcy shrugged. "I don't think so," she said.

"What's the matter?" Mark asked. "I thought we had it all planned."

She just shrugged again. "I don't know," she said. "I've just been thinking a lot about commitments lately, I guess. I've got to get to class. The tardy bell's about to ring."

Mark went to class, too — English. Mr. Santos wasn't there, which normally would have made Mark very happy, but the substitute switched from horror to a unit on nineteenth-century essays. The whole class wished for Santos back, but no one knew where he was or why he wasn't at school.

Ignoring the substitute's lecture, Mark thought about his conversation with Marcy. Commitment? he thought. Darn that Todd! This is all because he and Libby have been getting along so well and Marcy knows I'm not planning to go steady. I thought we had that worked out.

He finally cornered Marcy in the hall at the end of the day. "I thought we had that all worked out," he said. "You know how I feel about going steady."

"Yeah," she said. "You want to have as many girls available to you as possible. And you don't want to have to promise anyone anything. Maybe I want someone a little more mature than that."

Mark sighed to himself as he walked home. The afternoon was unexpectedly warm, the sky deep blue and cloudless. You figure her out, he told himself. You're the expert. Mark Carney, girl expert. Everyone should ask me for advice. I know everything about girls, except how to get along with them, how to get along without them, and how to understand them. And I can't even worry about Marcy right now because I've got a date with Janine.

Chapter 24

Mark drove automatically, thinking about what would happen later at the zoo. He was glad he hadn't eaten. As nervous as he was, he knew his stomach would be churning knots around any food he put into it.

"Hi," he told Janine. She'd run outside as soon as he'd parked. He barely had time to get out and open the car door for her before she reached it. "Are you in a hurry?" he asked. "Am I late?" He started the car and pulled away from the curb.

"I'm always in a hurry to get away from home," she said. "Besides, I was anxious to see Max. I knew he was impatiently awaiting me." She patted the dashboard. "Hi, Maxie," she said. She looked at Mark. "Hi to you, too," she added.

"You and Max seem to have something going on that I didn't know about," Mark said. "I'm not sure I approve."

"I'm not sure you get a vote," she said, laughing.

Mark merged smoothly onto the highway.

"It's a good thing we're not going the other way," Janine said. "Look at that. Everybody's going home at once. They call this rush hour? Nobody's moving."

"I almost wish we were going the other way," he muttered. "Then we'd be late. We'd miss him."

"I know," Janine said. "I'm kind of scared, too. But I want to do this. Even if we don't find anything out and nobody else ever knows, we will. I'll know I had something hard to do that I didn't want to do, and I did it even though I was scared."

She switched the radio on, but then, as if she was remembering the news she'd heard the last time, she switched it back off. They rode in silence to the zoo, lost in their own worries.

Mark paid their entrance fees and Janine grabbed his hand, holding it so hard it was almost numb by the time they reached the penguins. Mark carried the blanket under his other arm.

"Where's a good place to spread this out?" he asked. "I want to be near enough to rush to your aid if it's necessary, but far enough away so I don't look suspicious and scare him off."

Janine picked a spot and they spread the blanket out, then spread themselves out on it. "This wasn't the best disguise," Janine said thoughtfully. "It's getting cold. And it'll be getting dark by five-thirty. You're not going to look exactly inconspicuous lying here reading in the dark and freezing."

Mark wrapped his arms around her, pulling

her close. "I won't freeze this way," he said.

"I won't be keeping you warm, remember?" she said. "I'm going to be warming that bench over there by the penguins."

"How's he going to know it's you?" Mark asked.

Janine touched the blue ribbon she'd tied around her low ponytail. "This," she said.

Slowly Mark reached out and pulled the ribbon from her hair. He unwound the hairband and pulled it loose. Then he fluffed her hair around her shoulders.

"Why?" Janine asked.

"We can watch for him together, from here," Mark said. "You said I'd look suspicious lying here alone reading in the dark, but I won't look at all suspicious cuddled in a blanket with you. We can watch together."

"But how will we know it's the right guy?" Janine asked.

"How would we have known anyway? We'd only have been sure if he tried to snatch you, and I'm not willing to have you snatched."

"I might learn something talking to him," she said.

Mark shook his head. He put Janine's ribbon in his pocket. "At first I thought if he tried to hustle you into going somewhere else we could be suspicious of him. Then I realized anyone would probably do that. I probably would. Whether he's a kidnapper or not, he'll be trying to impress you, and will definitely be careful to not seem weird or scary. I don't think you'd learn all that much by talking to him, and I'm certainly not going to let you go anywhere with him."

"Then what good is it doing to even be here?" she asked. "What good will it do to see him from a distance and then let him walk away? We won't have accomplished anything."

"Ssh," Mark hissed. He tugged the blanket up around their shoulders, watching out of the corner of his eye as a short, thick man wearing a hat and an overcoat strolled past the penguins. He barely glanced in their direction, seeming more interested in the empty bench in front of the penguin cave.

"It's him," Mark whispered. "He did come early. He makes the hair on the back of my neck stand up. He's creepy!"

He kissed her, repositioning himself at the same time so they could both see the man without directly facing him.

"He's just a person," Janine whispered back. "Maybe he just wants to watch the penguins. He's too early to be Ben."

The man walked to the bench and sat down with his back to them.

"It's him," Mark insisted in a whisper. "He's the one. I know he is." He shuddered, certain he could feel evil rolling from the stranger across the space that separated them.

"Did you see his face?" she asked.

"I can't see very well from this distance," Mark said. "But there's something about him that looks familiar."

"Could we move closer?"

"Yeah, let's," Mark said.

They stood and folded the blanket together, wrapping their arms around each other. They made their way slowly towards the man, stopping often to kiss and watch him surreptitiously.

Two children walked by the bench and the man leaned forward, towards them. "Have you kids seen a young lady?" he called to them. "With a hair ribbon? A blue one?"

The children shook their heads.

"Something must have happened to her, then," he said, half to them, half to himself. "I hope she's okay. I hope it wasn't a problem of some kind."

He glanced apologetically at the kids. "Sorry to bother you," he said.

Mark whispered to Janine, "That voice sounds so familiar. It must be Ben. I've heard him talk before. If only I could see his face."

Almost as if he'd been listening, the figure on the bench stood up and took a few nervous steps in one direction, then in another. He took off his hat and brushed his hair back from his forehead with one hand. Then he turned and looked straight at Mark.

If Mark hadn't been holding tight to Janine, he'd have fallen over in surprise. "Todd!" he cried. "What are you doing here?"

Chapter 25

"I just don't seem to have much luck with girls," was Todd's explanation. It was several minutes later and they were sitting on the bench together.

"What about Libby?" Mark asked. "I thought you two were a couple."

"I thought so, too," Todd said. "But this week she started acting really strange. When I tried talking to her about it, she said she and Marcy were tired of meeting boys and she knew where to meet men. I don't know what she was talking about and she wouldn't explain. We were supposed to go out Wednesday, but I waited and waited and she never showed up."

"Who were you meeting tonight?" Janine asked gently. "Was it Libby?"

Todd shook his head. "Promise you won't tell anyone?" he asked. "It's a little embarrassing to talk about, but there's this thing on the phone called the Party Line."

Mark gave Janine a quick look behind Todd's back. Todd didn't notice.

"Before I met Libby I used it all the time," Todd said. "I never actually met anyone but it's a great way to talk to girls. And I need all the help I can get. After Libby stood me up on Wednesday, I started calling the Party Line again, and there was this really nice girl on. We agreed to meet here tonight. I guess I'm going for some kind of record. This is the second time this week I've been stood up."

It was nearly six-thirty when they headed for the exit. The parking lot was nearly empty, as the zoo had been. Mark and Janine watched as Todd unlocked the door of his father's car and drove off.

"Brother!" Mark said. "My own best friend!" I can't believe I thought I could feel evil rolling across the air! he thought. My imagination was really working overtime!

"This is pretty disappointing," Janine said. "I thought we were going to catch Ben and he was going to turn out to be the kidnapper. We caught Ben, all right. And he was just a harmless little mouse! He sure doesn't talk the same way in person as he did on the Line! If he'd just be himself, he'd have pretty good luck with girls. He's a nice guy."

"I still can't believe that Ben turned out to be Todd," Mark said. "No wonder I thought his voice sounded familiar! I thought for a while that he was Mr. Santos. How dumb can I get?"

"Should we have told him who I am?" Janine asked.

"No. He was in bad enough shape already. I

didn't want to destroy him. We'd have had to do a lot more explaining than I was prepared to do. How could I tell my best friend you arranged to meet him because he sounded like an oily-voiced jerk?"

"Do you think he could have had anything to do with the missing girls?"

"No," Mark said. "I've known Todd all my life. There's no way he's involved in this."

"Well, that takes care of Ben," Janine said. "But there are other oily guys on the Line. I'll try again later tonight. Maybe I'll get that Robert that Nicky was talking to. If I make a date, I'll let you know."

"With my luck it'll be someone else I know," Mark said. "If Ben is my friend Todd, then Robert will turn out to be my other good friend, Robbie."

They decided to make an early night of it so Janine could call the Line again. Mark dropped her off at her place and headed home.

If Todd was using the Line and I didn't even know it, then who else is? Mark wondered, looking for a snack in the kitchen. He grabbed a handful of cookies. There could be tons of people I know talking on the Line, he thought. Maybe I know them all. I could be talking with friends all the time and never know it.

He thought of the two girls he'd heard talking on the Line. Girl number 1 and girl number 2. It seemed so long ago now, but he remembered thinking one of them sounded like Libby. Could it have been? he asked himself. And did Libby get Marcy to start calling? Are those the more mature guys Libby was talking about?

That would be pretty funny, Mark thought, if everybody I know is calling the Line, now that I've quit!

Chapter 26

"Hey, Mark," Robbie said, just before the auto mechanics class on Saturday. He seemed a little nervous.

"Yeah?" Mark said. He eyed his friend cautiously, wondering vaguely if he could be a kidnapper. I'm the one who should be nervous, he thought. This is my first class. Robbie went over the lesson plans with me, but I'm still a little shaky about teaching.

"Uh, I have to make a few phone calls," Robbie said. "Privately. Do you think you could cover for me in class for a while?" Robbie lowered his voice. "I know I always act like meeting girls is easy," he said. "But we've been friends a long time, and I can tell you. It isn't always as easy as I make it sound. Sometimes you have to rely on less usual ways of meeting girls."

Robbie looked around nervously, as if checking to be sure no one else could hear his confession. "I think I've finally met someone special," he said. "She sounds really nice, anyway. I've been trying to get ahold of her for a date tonight and I've been leaving messages all over the place. I need to see if she got them."

He grinned shyly, and Mark suddenly knew for certain that Robbie would never hurt anyone. He was embarrassed that he'd ever been suspicious of his friend. "Of course I'll cover for you," he said. "But tell me, what did you mean by less usual ways of meeting girls?"

Robbie flushed. "Nothing," he said.

Mark started the lesson, explaining drums and shoes and cylinders, covering theory and then removing wheels to let the class discover what was actually going on behind their tires.

The time was almost over, the students cleaning and replacing tools, when the phone rang, startling Mark. He hadn't realized the shop had a phone in the back.

One of the women answered it, then held it out to Mark. "For you," she said.

Mark finished wiping his hands and took the phone.

"This is Mark," he said.

"Oh, Mark! I've been talking to Robert," Janine said. "I called the Line and got the message he was looking for me, so I kept calling in and I just got him. He wants to go out tonight! What do you think?"

"I don't believe this!" Mark said, laughing. "The pieces all just fell into place, Janine. You just made a date with one of my best friends.

Some girlfriend you are, two-timing me with my best buddy."

"You're kidding!" Janine said.

"I'm serious," Mark assured her. "He's been walking around on a cloud about his maybe new girlfriend. He's also been gone for the last hour, phoning her. What do you think? Am I kidding? Is this coincidence?"

"I said I'd meet him at Cowley Park at five-thirty. I wasn't going to show up unless you could be there, but I wanted to make the arrangements so I could tell you where and when to go. I have to leave right now to catch the bus if I'm going, but if he's your friend I don't see the point. So what do I do?"

"You keep the date, I guess," Mark said. "I'm not telling Robbie that his new girl is my old girl. You'll have to."

"I could just not show up," Janine said.

"Uh-uh," Mark told her, still laughing. "I helped you stand Todd up last night. I'm not helping you do the same thing to Robbie tonight! It just wouldn't be fair. You'll just have to go and have a good time — but not too good of a time! — and then tell him the truth."

"What if the truth turns out to be that I like him better?" Janine asked.

"No way," Mark said. "He's a nice guy, but not that nice. The problem is he's really looking forward to tonight, and I don't have the heart to spoil it for him. Once he knows the truth he'll want to strangle me, but he'll see the humor, too, I'm sure."

"Okay," Janine said. "But just remember, it was your idea. You can't call me a two-timer if it was your idea."

Mark finished cleaning the classroom, then hurried outside, heading towards the building where the self-defense class was held. As he rounded the corner, Robbie drove by in his Chevy. Mark almost laughed out loud.

"Thanks for covering for me!" Robbie shouted. "I got ahold of her and we're on for tonight. And guess what? She knows you! Isn't that wild?"

"Have fun at Cowley Park!" Mark yelled back.

"Cowley Park? What's that? We're going to a movie."

"With Janine?" Mark called.

Robbie was farther away, but Mark could still hear his answer, "Who's Janine? Her name's Marcy!"

Marcy? Mark thought, feeling suddenly bleak and very cold. Robbie's going out with Marcy? Then who . . . ?

Chapter 27

Mark ran back to the auto mechanics shed and grabbed the phone, his stomach feeling like it was loaded with acid pellets, and his heart thudding.

He called Janine.

"Be there!" he said out loud, waiting through twenty rings even though he knew she was already gone. "Be there!"

Then someone picked up the phone.

"Janine!" Mark yelled. "Stop! Don't — "

"Hello?" said a female voice. "Who did you ask for?"

"Janine," Mark said.

"There's no Janine at this number."

"Is this 555-1212?" Mark asked.

"Yes, it is. But there's no Janine here." And the phone clicked, the line dead.

The sound of the dial tone began its ominous hum in Mark's ear.

For a moment Mark's brain came to a complete stop.

If Robbie isn't Robert then Janine is in trouble.

But if Janine isn't Janine . . . then I'm crazy.

He pushed the thought to the back of his mind.

I know one thing for sure, he told himself. Someone is in danger. And if I don't get to Cowley Park in about two minutes, something terrible is going to happen.

Chapter 28

Mark grabbed the phone book and the notepad and pen that dangled from nails in the wall by the phone. He scribbled down the name of the park as he thumbed madly through the C's in the book. There was no Cowley Park listed.

Oh, no, he thought. Parks don't have phones. He tried the yellow pages of the book, finding a listing for Parks but none for Cowley.

Wait, he thought. Cowley Park could be on Cowley Street, if there is such a street. Isn't there? There must be!

He turned to the back of the phone book, exhaling sharply in relief when he found a street guide. He found Cowley Avenue, looked it up on the map and followed it, finding a Cowley Lake but no park.

There aren't any parks on this map! he realized. They'd be shaded green or something if there were any! He was shaking now, from fear and frustration.

Think! he ordered himself. Panic won't help Janine!

He slumped to the floor, holding the useless phone book. Who would know? he asked himself.

Wait a minute. Lake. Cowley Lake. There's got to be a park there!

He leapt to his feet, dropping the book. He picked it back up and looked up Scotty's Pizza, where his mother had said the gas station was where she'd leave the car. He found the address, breathed, "Thank you!" when he realized he knew where it was, and then ran. He ran out of the shed and tore off up the street.

He ran block after block, his heart pounding from both the exertion and his fear.

Bus! he told himself, panting. You can't run all the way there. It's miles. Find a bus!

As if on command a large, white snub-nosed bus slid across the intersection ahead of him. Mark ran after it, yelling, but it pulled away from the empty bus stop without even slowing down.

"Hey!" Mark yelled after it.

"He won't wait for anybody."

Mark jerked around, seeing a small gray-haired woman with a large, shiny red purse.

"If you're two seconds late he drives off," she said.

"I've got to get to Scotty's Pizza," Mark said. "On Clayborne near Main. I've got to get there fast!"

"You won't get there at all on that bus," she said, glancing after the disappearing public transport.

"When's the next one?" Mark asked, his breath slowing, but his panic growing stronger again.

"Soon," she said. "You wait. Calm down, honey. Jumping around won't get you there any faster."

"Does the next bus go to Main?" he asked.

"No," she said.

"Oh, no!" Mark said dumbly, feeling despair again.

"It'll turn west about eight blocks before Main," she went on calmly, as if showing him by example how to wait patiently for a bus. "You can get off at the far end of the mall and then walk the eight blocks up to Main. Clayborne's two blocks east of Main."

"Oh, thank you!" Mark said. "When will the bus be here?"

"A few more minutes, young man," she said. "She must be awfully pretty for you to get so riled up about. Will she wait for you if you're late?"

"I don't know," Mark said, fear creeping back into his voice.

"You don't look terribly gussied up for her," the old woman observed. "Greasy and sweaty. That about sums you up."

Mark looked blankly at the coveralls he hadn't removed. He just shook his head. It didn't matter. Nothing mattered except finding Janine — before . . .

Before that Robert person meets her? There's not much chance of getting there before they meet, he realized. I've got to find her before he kidnaps her — or kills her.

He swallowed hard against the knot in his throat. He's the one, he thought. I sent Janine straight to the guy who's been luring girls to meet him and then kidnapping them. What does he do with them? They never show up again. Does he kill them? Mark had a terrible, gnawing fear that Janine was in serious danger. He felt little else except a desperate need to move, to find her, to be sure she was okay.

"Here it is, honey. You go first. You're in the biggest hurry."

The bus slowed to a stop, the door hissing open. Mark dropped a handful of change in the coin box, found a seat and waited, cursing inwardly at each stop. His feet tapped nervously against the metal floor, his fingers drumming on the plastic cover of the seat ahead of him. He clenched his teeth. He shivered.

At the far end of the mall he was up, waiting, as the bus slowed, stopped. He leaped to the sidewalk, ignoring the bus steps, and took off, counting the blocks as he ran. He prayed that the old woman had given him good directions, prayed that his mother had left the car somewhere obvious, prayed that Janine was still okay, still breathing, still alive.

Be alive! he chanted silently. Be alive! Janine, be alive! Please be alive!

The eighth block from the Mall was Main, and Mark turned east, breathing deeply, the breaths keeping time with the refrain in his mind. Be alive! Please be alive!

The second block to the east was Clayborne. There was Scotty's, right where it should be, with a gas station to its left on the corner. And another gas station across from that one, and a third on the corner opposite Mark.

After only a second's pause Mark ran across to the station opposite him, and still running as fast as he could, circled the building. No Max. He ran across the next intersection against the light, pausing only to wait for a break in traffic. His breath rasped and his sides hurt.

He almost sobbed aloud when he saw Max's familiar boxy shape squatting patiently at the rear of the station. He knew he'd never seen anything more beautiful in his life. He fumbled through the slit in his coveralls, reaching into his pockets for the car keys.

He had Max unlocked and started in seconds, sighing with relief at how smoothly the engine turned over.

Now, he thought blankly. Which way to Cowley?

Somehow his brain supplied him with directions and he drove automatically, his arms, eyes and feet taking care of the mechanics of speeding up, slowing down, turning, watching for traffic while his mind raced as fast as his heart, spinning, pounding, but not providing him with a plan. All he knew was that he had to find Janine. He didn't know how he would help her once he found her — if he found her at all.

His mind veered from that thought.

Finally there was the entrance to the lake. The sign read, "Cowley Park, open to the public. Cowley Lake, closed for the season. Park hours 7 A.M. to 9 P.M. Sun. - Thurs. 7 A.M. to 11 P.M. Fri. & Sat. No glass. No pets. No vehicles beyond lot."

And none there, either, Mark thought, scanning the empty parking lot. He drove in and turned around, his heart suddenly heavy in his chest. He stopped the car and slumped, folding his arms on the steering wheel, letting his head fall into his forearms. He was beyond tears.

I didn't find her, he thought in despair. I was too late. She's dead. And it's all my fault.

Chapter 29

"Are you sick, too?"

The voice meant nothing to Mark, though he could hear it clearly through the open window. He didn't move.

"I said, are you sick, too?"

The voice was nearer, and dimly Mark realized that a child was speaking to him. He looked up, out the window at a little boy who stood looking curiously at him. The boy held a skateboard in his arms and was spinning one wheel with his fingers. It made a ratchety, whirring sound.

"I guess everybody's getting sick," the boy said. "First her and now you. Only she had somebody helping her. Who's going to help you? Not me. I can't drive. But if I could drive, I'd drive a cool car."

Mark stared blankly at the child.

"You don't have a cool car," he said. "Jeeps aren't cool. Especially old Jeeps like this one. Neither are Bugs. I'd drive a TransAm. Or a Corvette. Not a dumb Bug."

"Did you see a Bug?" Mark asked, astonished. He felt a tiny flare of hope that he might yet find Janine.

The boy looked disgusted. "Didn't I just say so?" he asked.

"Here?"

"Yeah, here. A gray Bug. I told you. He helped her into it."

"Because she was sick?" Mark prompted eagerly.

"Yeah. She looked like she was gonna barf. You know, holding her stomach and her face all white and funny-looking."

"Was she a high school girl?" Mark asked. "Kind of tall with brownish hair?"

"Yeah," the boy agreed. "And he musta been her dad or maybe her big brother, 'cause he was being awful nice. I wouldn't help someone if they were going to barf. They might barf on me."

"Did you see where they went?" Mark almost held his breath waiting for the boy to answer. He wanted to reach out and shake the information from him, but he knew that wouldn't produce the results as fast as waiting for the answer. He bit his tongue and clamped his jaw to keep from screaming at the child.

"I did think that was funny," the kid said, scratching his head with the hand that wasn't spinning the skateboard wheels. "They went that way." He pointed to a graveled road that curved away from the road Mark had come on, almost like an exit aiming back parallel to the park and lake.

"They're just building that road," the boy explained. "There's no houses there, and no hospital. If she was sick, why did he take her up there? There's just dump trucks and stuff."

Mark shouted his thanks to the startled boy as he started the engine, gunning it. He spun gravel into the air as he sped out of the park and onto the road the boy had pointed out. Mark glanced in his rearview mirror and saw the child trudge off, presumably heading for home. The sun was just setting over the mountains to the west.

Since it was still light enough to see without them, Mark left his headlights off, not wanting to give any unnecessary warning of his approach.

The boy was right, there were no houses. The road was little more than a dirt path leading around a couple of sharp corners, then up and down through what looked like a dirt-bike course. The city lights came on in the distance as Mark climbed steadily upward, the pace painfully slow due to the ruts and holes. Frustrated, bursting with fear, Mark gritted his teeth and banged the steering wheel as he drove.

I'll never get there in time, he thought. Why didn't I ask the kid how long ago they drove up here? What did he do to make her look pale and sick? Be okay, Janine. Please be okay!

He made his way as fast as he could, but still slowly, always climbing upward. Even if the road wound down a ways, it always twisted back and up again, giving him a clear view of the city spread out below each time he topped a rise. He glanced around. He seemed to be skirting what would one day be a large housing development overlooking the city. There were clumps of cleared spaces for buildings linked by half-excavated streets. A few plots had flags marking boundaries or driveways or foundations.

Mark thought it looked ghostly in the fading light, the excavated land looming like pale patches against the darker, undisturbed soil of the hillside. He shivered again, a shiver partly of fear, and partly from the chilly night air blowing in through the still-open window.

After the construction area the road angled right, towards the wooded portion of the hill. The road was barely a path now and Mark had trouble seeing it as dusk deepened the shadows and faded the colors from the land. But he didn't want to use his headlights and give a warning of his arrival. He leaned forward, peering through the trees to see where he was headed.

The scream came clearly across the evening air, making Mark's skin prickle with fear. It was a scream made from the word NO, but filled with despair. Suddenly Mark saw a gray Volkswagen pulled off to the side of the path and half-hidden among the trees.

Mark slammed the Jeep to a stop behind the VW and leaped out, racing through the woods towards whatever he might find.

Chapter 30

It was darker in the woods and Mark stumbled, whacking his shin sharply on unseen branches. He scrambled to his feet and ran on, driven by the emotion he'd heard in Janine's scream.

There was no time for thought — thought was too rational and orderly for such a desperate situation. Thought would have told him he was running to probable death, would have made him pause, would have reduced him to a frightened boy. Instead he was a missile, aimed and guided, thrust from his car towards the far edge of the small woods, intent only on speed.

He saw a shadowy hulk rise from the ground in alarm as he approached. One part of Mark's mind noted the pale figure of the girl, lying too still, but he didn't process the information. He flew across the last few feet between him and the man's bulk, screaming as he'd screamed in his self-defense classes. He lashed out with his hands and feet, aiming for the vulnerable spots, going for blood. He whirled and slashed, feeling the jar of each blow as it connected. There was no hesitation in his attack for he had no thought that it was a man he was attacking. If he had thought at all, it would have been of protecting a friend, but he did not think. He simply acted.

Suddenly his head exploded and he fell into a blackened, silent world. For a time he could remember nothing, for nothing had any reality. He hovered in the black silence, vaguely aware that if he moved, pain would come crashing over him along with . . . along with what? There were no words. He asked himself the question but not as a question. He simply became aware of a small area of doubt in his mind. Slowly the area of doubt enlarged, formed into a picture of a too-still form lying on the ground.

Janine, he thought. But the thought, desperate as it was, couldn't provide impetus as it had before. Mark found himself incapable of moving. It was as if the blow had short-circuited him, leaving him suspended in a curious, disconnected half-world.

Then he felt something. It was the first sensation other than a dull awareness of hovering pain that he'd felt since the blow, and it took a moment for him to realize that someone had ahold of one of his ankles and was dragging him along over the ground. His head bounced and thumped.

The pain set in all over then, washing through him, bringing reality back in waves as if someone stood at the world's control knob twirling it way up, then way down, then back up again.

Mark's stomach revolted against the pain, adding nausea to the ebb and flow of feeling. The nausea, pain and noise served to unite his awareness and he knew he was conscious. Gingerly he tried moving his arms, thinking vaguely of halting the bouncing of his head.

In a massive wave of pain, he fainted.

When he woke next his left arm felt numb, his head pounded with a throbbing ache and he could barely open one of his eyes. He was aware of a rattling, gasping noise that he finally identified as muted sobbing coming from somewhere inside his own throat. Next he realized he was also hearing a string of muttered curses, and that he could feel someone ripping roughly at his clothes.

He looked up. Finally he would get to see the face that had haunted his dreams for the last month.

He saw the short, slim body. It's not Robbie, he thought, vastly relieved even though he'd already known it couldn't be Robbie.

He saw the straight blond hair. It's not Mr. Santos after all, he thought.

He saw the jagged scar on the forehead.

Pieces fell into place.

It's Vince, Mark realized. He's stuffed us both into the Volkswagen. Janine is behind me. I know she's alive because she's crying. And Vince is trying to find my car keys. I parked Max behind him. He can't get away.

He could quit pawing at me, Mark thought, the first prickles of anger returning. I left the keys in Max. They aren't in my pocket. I didn't have time for that. I was in a hurry. I wanted to help Janine. I wasn't much help. But she's alive. She's still alive.

Evidently Vince realized that Mark didn't have the keys for he finally quit searching and Mark both heard and felt the Volkwagen's door slam shut.

Now, he told himself. It's now or never.

He ordered himself to move, but it was like trying to zip boots and fasten buttons with bulky gloves on, for nothing responded precisely to his orders. He managed to orient himself, figuring out that he was in the cramped backseat of the VW. He worked his way into a crouch and clambered awkwardly through the space between the two front seats, trying not to climb on Janine's head. He lurched, his left arm flapping uselessly, but at least it was mostly numb and no longer creating the sharp waves of pain. His left leg felt like it was on fire and moved reluctantly, not quite flapping as his arm did, but still with its motion impaired.

Dimly Mark heard Max start.

He looked at the Volkswagen's dashboard. The engine was rumbling gently, the headlights aimed into the grove of trees. With a clumsy, unresponsive leg Mark managed to ease the clutch in and slowly, quietly put the gearshift lever into reverse. He peered out the window, thinking the glass was oddly blurred and smeared until he realized it was his own vision that was blurred.

Abruptly Vince gunned Max's engine and backed the Jeep quickly out of the way.

"Now!" Mark told himself. But his left leg had grown half-numb and the foot seemed like a lead weight. It wouldn't respond. The clutch stayed firmly pressed to the floor. Mark watched in frozen horror as Vince climbed from Max's front seat.

We're dead, Mark thought.

Suddenly Vince drew his arm back, still standing near the Jeep, and then made a throwing motion. Mark saw a tiny glitter in the moonlight.

He threw the keys away! Mark thought. It took several more long seconds before Mark realized that without keys, Vince couldn't chase him. But Vince was chasing him! He'd begun a long-striding lope towards the little car, not yet noticing that Mark was behind the wheel.

In panic Mark revved the engine. His numbed foot responded sluggishly, falling off the clutch pedal. The Volkswagen leaped backward, clipping Vince's leg as he reached for the door handle.

Vince roared something incomprehensible, a bellow of surprised rage. He grabbed for the handle, then scrabbled for a handhold on the bumper as Mark worked the clutch in one more time, and with the engine revving jammed the gearshift lever into second, bypassing first for the speed advantage of second gear. He knew he could start out in second if he gave the car enough gas. He let his foot fall back off the clutch and the car jerked forward, lurching by the prone figure of Vince. He scrambled to his feet as Mark passed him.

Mark blinked furiously, trying to clear his vision. He bounced through and across the ruts in the road, the car jouncing violently. He could barely keep his one-handed grip on the steering wheel, but didn't dare slow down.

Janine moaned from the backseat and Mark had a vivid picture in his mind of her being thrown from side to side on this wild ride, smashing already broken limbs, breaking open freshly-clotted wounds and bleeding slowly to death while Mark struggled through the darkness, caught in a nightmare of trying to drive to safety with a numbed arm and leg, pounding head, blurred vision and a madman running behind him.

He slewed the car around the first gentle curve, engine screaming in protest. You have to shift, Mark told himself. But knowing that he had to do it didn't translate into the ability to do it. He'd barely managed to shift while the car was stopped. With it bouncing along it seemed impossible. His left arm simply ignored all commands, and the ruts in the road made steering one-handed difficult enough — every time the car jounced, the wheel jerked violently, taking all of Mark's dwindling strength to simply maintain his hold.

Slowly he maneuvered his unresponsive leg up, over towards the clutch pedal. It was growing more numb and the only feeling was an odd tingling sensation. He couldn't tell if his foot touched the pedal or not. He tried again with the same result, grimly controlling the steering wheel while he worked his leg.

He glanced hurriedly in the rearview mirror and sobbed aloud. Even with blurred vision he could see the limping man gaining on the little car. Mark jammed his foot harder on the gas pedal but the engine protested with a loud screaming whine. It couldn't go any faster. He had to shift into a higher gear if he was going to pick up speed.

Dummy! Mark shrieked at himself mentally. You can shift without the clutch! Just match your engine and transmission speeds!

He eased off the gas pedal and yanked the gearshift into neutral. He revved the gas once and eased off, listening to the engine. He leaned his chest and knee against the steering wheel to hold it steady, then grabbed the shifter with his good hand. When he judged the timing was right he slid the gearshift lever towards third gear. It balked, grinding, but as the engine slowed more, it clunked into gear.

Mark nearly wept in relief, immediately punching the gas and grabbing the steering wheel with his right arm again. The little car shot forward, hit a bump and the wheel spun out of his hand. They careened towards the edge of the ridge overlooking town.

"No!" Mark shouted. What good does it do to rescue Janine and then run her off a cliff? he thought wildly. He yanked the car back from the edge of the road, but the detour had given Vince the advantage. He leaped to the top of the car, his body spread across it from side to side, holding on to the luggage rack with his fingertips curling down into the car on the driver's side.

"Gah!" Mark yelled. He tried to roll up the window but his left arm wouldn't cooperate and he couldn't let go of the steering wheel with the other arm to reach across and fumble with the winding knob.

In what seemed like slow motion the fingers worked their way farther into the car.

Oh, no! Mark thought. It's the nightmares all over again!

In horror he realized the man was humming loudly enough to be heard over the noise of the car — a sound insanely happy in contrast to the terror of Mark's reality. The tune was hauntingly familiar, but Mark couldn't place it.

It took him a moment to realize it didn't matter what song it was. I'm going crazy, he thought.

Evidently Vince shifted and found a secure grip on the luggage rack, holding on with one hand, for his left hand suddenly lurched through the window, grabbing Mark's shoulder.

Mark screamed. His left arm may have been numb but his shoulder wasn't, nor was his sense of fear. He screamed again, then bent his head to the side and bit Vince's hand as hard as he could. He set his jaw and jerked his head back and forth, trying to bite clear through the hand and rip it apart.

It's a bloody arm, Mark thought dimly. The bloody arm. It's going to kill me.

The fingers gripped deeper into his shoulder in response to Mark's teeth, but Mark only bit harder. Then, just as the hand let loose of his shoulder, the car hit a deep dip and stopped completely, the steering wheel ripping itself from Mark's hand. With only instinct left to guide him, Mark yanked the gearshift into neutral to keep the car from stalling. He didn't think he would have the time or the strength to get it started again if it stalled. Then he punched the gas pedal, eased off and slid into first gear. He needed the low power of first gear to get out of the rut more than he needed the speed of second gear.

The Volkswagen shuddered violently and climbed abruptly out of the dip. Vince, his balance already precarious from the sudden stop, slid off the roof, down the driver's side, grabbing for something to stop his fall. His fingers raking Mark's cheek, Vince flipped over in the air, tumbling to the ground.

Mark sped up quickly, made it into second gear and was suddenly on the straight section of the road, speeding downhill past the ghostly construction site. Vince was nowhere to be seen.

Mark wept in relief, the tears blurring his vision even more.

It's too quiet in the backseat, he thought numbly. But he was too afraid to stop so he could check on Janine. He was afraid Vince would reappear if he stopped. He was afraid that Janine would be dead, and he didn't want to discover that. He decided their best chance was to drive straight to a hospital. He slipped into third gear and kept driving as fast as he could.

With the immediate terror of Vince behind him, Mark's body made a sudden clamor, telling him it had been ignored too long. His head throbbed, the eye that wouldn't open fully itched, burned and ached all at the same time. His left arm sent needle-sharp messages of agony up through the damaged shoulder and his chest protested with every breath. His stomach was still nauseated and there didn't seem to be a single square inch of himself, inside or out, that felt normal and free of pain. His stomach heaved sharply.

You can't barf, he told himself. He let go of the steering wheel briefly, bracing it with his right knee while he wiped the sweat from his forehead. His hand came away sticky, leaving a black smear of blood on the wheel when he grabbed it again.

Suddenly he remembered the sharp curves ahead, near the exit back into the park. His left leg still responded sluggishly, hurting now instead of feeling numb. He kicked it aside with his right leg, fumbling with his foot for the brake. The first curve loomed ahead and though the car had slowed when he let off the gas, it still seemed to Mark that he was going much too fast.

He glanced in the rearview mirror, seeing humanoid shadows chasing him, arms reaching for the car. He blinked hard, but his vision didn't clear. Now the shadows were coming at him from the sides, too, huge limping shadows with blood dripping from them.

He yanked the wheel sideways to escape one and drove straight towards another. He slowed even more, one foot fighting the other as he tried to find the brake. He spun around the last curve and gasped at the red and blue lightning, the white shooting stars.

I'm dead, he thought.

Though he didn't realize it, his foot found the brake and pressed against it, slowing the car till it was barely creeping along. Since he didn't push in the clutch or pull the shifter into neutral, the Volkswagen jerked and chugged, then stalled, engine dead.

Mark had stopped fifteen feet from three police cruisers and Robbie's Chevy, all of their lights shining directly at him, but he didn't know it. He didn't know anything. He was unconscious.

Afterwards

Mark sat in Max, in the passenger's seat, watching glumly as the white lines marking the center of the road whizzed by. The last few days had been cold and snowy but this morning was unexpectedly warm with bright sunshine. He had called Alise to come over early.

"Just drive," Mark had told her, so she had driven. They were twenty miles from the city now, heading east. Soon they would have to turn around and drive back.

Mark watched the countryside out of his window. The fields had been recently plowed, perhaps for a crop of spring or winter wheat. The scarred furrows rose and fell in gentle swells. The road climbed up and as they crested a small hill, the whole valley lay spread out in front of them.

"Pull over," Mark said.

Alise stopped the car and they looked in wonder at the farmland. Some trick of sunshine and cold earth, mixing with warmed air, had created a layer of wispy fog that hung suspended over the fields. They could see the dark earth beneath, then an eerie layer of mist, then the bright sky above that. And beyond the fog, poised for take-off but still tethered to the earth, a brilliantly colored hot-air balloon billowed in the morning air.

"Wow!" Alise whispered. "It's beautiful!"

"It is," Mark agreed quietly. His eyes were on the balloon but his thoughts rambled, pausing on one image, then another.

He saw his mother, looking worried and pale as she bent over his hospital bed.

He saw his own body beneath the hospital sheets, a livid map of black, purple, red, blue and yellow bruises from the kicks Vince had delivered while Mark was unconcious.

He saw the faces of Janine's parents breaking, sobbing as they said, "She's all right. He didn't hurt her, really. She's all right. Thank you." He saw Janine smiling as he woke up in the hospital, in a room filled with flowers.

"You really threw me with that Janine business," he told Alise.

"I already said I was sorry," she said.

"Even after I told you my real name, you just laughed," he reminded her. "You said you were still Janine!"

"I was going to tell you. I've always had trouble trusting people, and giving a false name just made sense. Everybody gives false names on the Line. But I'd already decided I could trust you. I was just waiting for the right moment. It's not easy admitting you've lied, you know. But I'm sorry my mom scared you so badly when you called and asked for Janine."

He blinked back tears at the memory of the frantic phone call. He'd been crying at odd times a lot these days.

Mark glanced briefly away from the balloon. "We have to testify Monday," he told Alise quietly. "It's a kind of pre-trial thing called a deposition where his lawyer will ask us all kinds of questions. We'll have a district attorney with us. It's the State against Vincent Benjamin Stevens. Criminal charges are always the State against somebody. At least that means we're just witnesses, not the plaintiff. We don't have to pay for a lawyer."

"I know," Alise said gently. "Will he be there?"

"Probably not," Mark said. "The D.A. said he won't be, anyway. I'm glad. I don't ever want to see him again. If it goes to trial we'll have to testify again."

"It might not go to trial?"

"If he fails his psychiatric examination he'll be put in an institution until he's able to stand trial. I hope that's how it works. He was obviously crazy, if you ask me. I can't believe someone would kidnap four girls just to keep them in his basement. That's crazy. It's just plain crazy."

"The other two missing girls have been found," Elise said. "Did you hear? One came home on her own, and one was found with a friend in California."

Mark lapsed into silence. The nightmares were coming a little less often now, and the school psychologist had suggested they'd stop faster if he could bring himself to talk about it as if it were just something else that had happened in his life.

"Get some distance from it," the psychologist had advised. "Time will help. So will talking. It wasn't personal. It wasn't an attack against Mark Carney. It was a tortured person's attack against a world he couldn't control, couldn't understand, and couldn't fit into. His 'best friend' that he told you about in class? That was his wife. She was with him when he was mugged, and he feels guilty that he couldn't save her. He couldn't deal with the guilt when it happened, but guilt doesn't go away. Traumas have to be dealt with or they'll come back to haunt you later. That's why you have to deal with your trauma now, Mark."

Mark thought about Vince. As they'd led him away in handcuffs he'd said, "I wasn't going to hurt anyone. I just wanted someone near me. People to talk to."

He wasn't really a monster, Mark thought sadly. Just a confused and lonely person. I was the only one he hurt physically, and that was just because I'd seen him. And I was trying to keep him from taking Janine. I thought she was dead, but he'd just knocked her out. Some trick with pressure points.

"I thought it was strange when you were late to class," Todd had told Mark in the hospital. "But I wasn't worried. I knew you had the mechanics class to teach and I figured you just got hung up with someone needing extra help. But Vince never came. And Marcy and Libby didn't come, either. Then finally Robbie showed up with Marcy and a wild tale about you yelling odd things at him. We didn't know what to think. We didn't know what was going on."

"I guess I didn't either, really," Mark had said. "Vince was all three of them, you know. Ben and Steve and Robert. Todd wasn't Ben after all. I had figured out something, but not what was really going on."

"You had just disappeared," Todd had said. "No one saw you go. No one knew where you went. Then we found that piece of paper with Cowley Park scribbled on it. It was all we had to go on and none of us even knew if you were the one who'd written it. We didn't know if it was your handwriting or not, but it was all we had."

"I'm glad you went after me," Mark said. "When I woke up . . . after I thought I'd been zapped by colored lightning, I saw Marcy and Robbie looking down at me, and I thought they were angels. I'm glad they found each other, Todd. I guess the main reason I couldn't make a commitment to Marcy was because I'd already made one . . . to Janine."

Todd had chuckled. "You should have heard Marcy when she yelled at the cops!" he said. "She was certain you were all in danger but they didn't want to go on a wild goose chase, as they called it. Marcy convinced them they'd better show up at the park or we'd all show up at the police station. I guess they didn't want that. When there wasn't anybody at the park we didn't know what to do next. And then you scared us even more rolling up in that Volkswagen and lurching to a stop right in front of us. We didn't know who it was."

"Just me and Janine," Mark had said. "You know, Detective Laker told me they'd finally had sense enough to get an advance listing of the toll calls made from Nicky's phone. Evidently she'd just started calling, and there were a lot of Party Line calls. They would have shown up on the next month's bill. So he'd about decided that I was on to something after all. They were going to check the bills of the other missing girls, too, when all this happened."

Mark looked over at Alise. "Remember I thought it might be Mr. Santos?" Mark said. "He'd disappeared and no one knew where he was. It turned out his wife had been in the hospital, having twins. No wonder he'd been so nervous and strange lately."

"I know," she said softly. "You told me, remember?"

"Oh, right," Mark said. "We've talked so much I keep forgetting what I've said and what I haven't."

They'd both tried to explore their feelings, comparing nightmares. Alise felt so badly for the girls Vince had locked in his basement, worse than she felt for herself. "Luckily they'll be all right," she'd said. "He didn't hurt them. They said he was always kind and polite. He really meant what he said. He just wanted someone around. He wanted a friend."

"Earth to Mark," came Alise's voice from next to him. "Are you there? Sign on and come in, please."

Slowly Mark grinned. He'd reminded Alise she'd never figured out a sign-on tone for him and she'd laughed. "I did, too," she said. "I gave you my phone number. You can sign on any time. It's the only sign-on tone you'll be needing. Especially now that you've got my name right."

"Look," Mark told Alise, pointing. The hot-air balloon was plumper now, rounder, straining skyward.

"Go!" Mark urged, his voice so low it was more like a breath of air than a word.

"Oh, go," he breathed. "Take off. Fly."

As he urged, the balloon strained harder, then lifted. Free of its restraining tethers it lifted higher, rising steadily until it was soaring in triumph above the mists.

Mark sighed softly. He smiled. He turned to Alise. "Okay," Mark said to his friend. "It's okay. We can go home now."

point

THRILLERS

It's a roller coaster of mystery, suspense, and excitement with **thrillers** from Scholastic's Point! Gripping tales that will keep you turning from page to page—strange happenings, unsolved mysteries, and things unimaginable!

Get ready for the ride of your life!

Other books you will enjoy,
about real kids like you!

☐ 42365-7	**Blind Date** R.L. Stine	$2.50
☐ 41248-5	**Double Trouble** Barthe DeClements and Christopher Greimes	$2.75
☐ 41432-1	**Just a Summer Romance** Ann M. Martin	$2.50
☐ 40935-2	**Last Dance** Caroline B. Cooney	$2.50
☐ 41549-2	**The Lifeguard** Richie Tankersley Cusick	$2.50
☐ 33829-3	**Life Without Friends** Ellen Emerson White	$2.75
☐ 40548-9	**A Royal Pain** Ellen Conford	$2.50
☐ 41823-8	**Simon Pure** Julian F. Thompson	$2.75
☐ 40927-1	**Slumber Party** Christopher Pike	$2.50
☐ 41186-1	**Son of Interflux** Gordon Korman	$2.50
☐ 41513-7	**The Tricksters** Margaret Mahy	$2.95
☐ 41546-8	**Yearbook II: Best All-Around Couple** Melissa Davis	$2.50

PREFIX CODE
0-590-

Available wherever you buy books...
or use the coupon below.